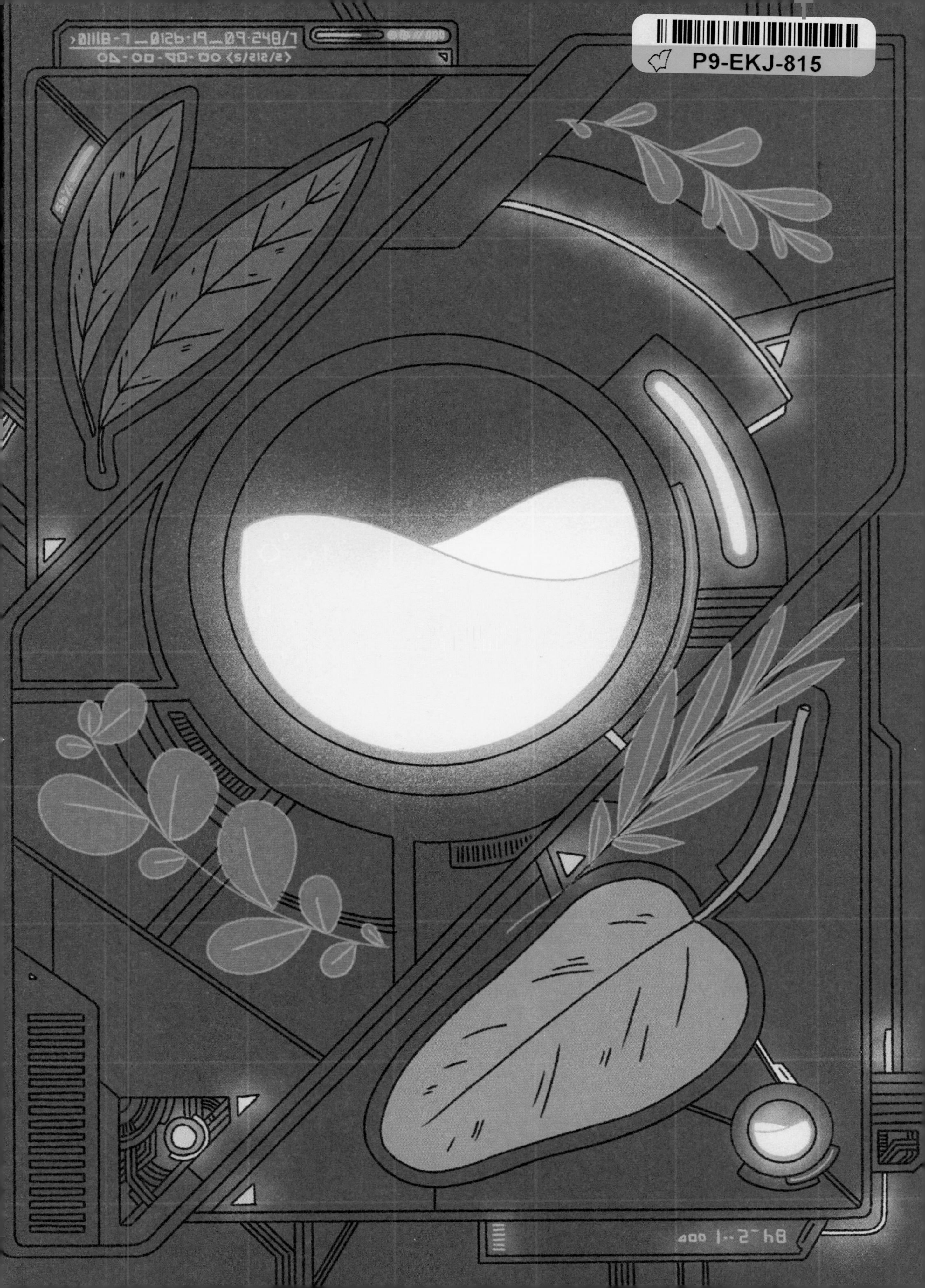

Dedicated to my parents, Lee, TaePoong, Hannah,
Keira & Maia, Tim, and to Nobrow/Flying Eye Books

First published in 2023 by Flying Eye Books,
An imprint of Nobrow Ltd. 27 Westgate Street, London, E8 3RL.

Concept and Illustrations © Sarah Soh 2023
Text © Tim Fraser 2023
Sarah Soh has asserted her right under the Copyright, Designs and Patents Act,
1988, to be identified as the Author and Illustrator of this Work.

1 3 5 7 9 10 8 6 4 2

Edited by Niamh Jones
Designed by Lilly Gottwald

Published in the US by Nobrow (US) Inc.
Printed in Poland on FSC® certified paper.

ISBN: 978-1-91249-745-4
www.flyingeyebooks.com

SARAH SOH

JUNIPER MAE

KNIGHT OF TYKOTECH CITY

FLYING EYE BOOKS

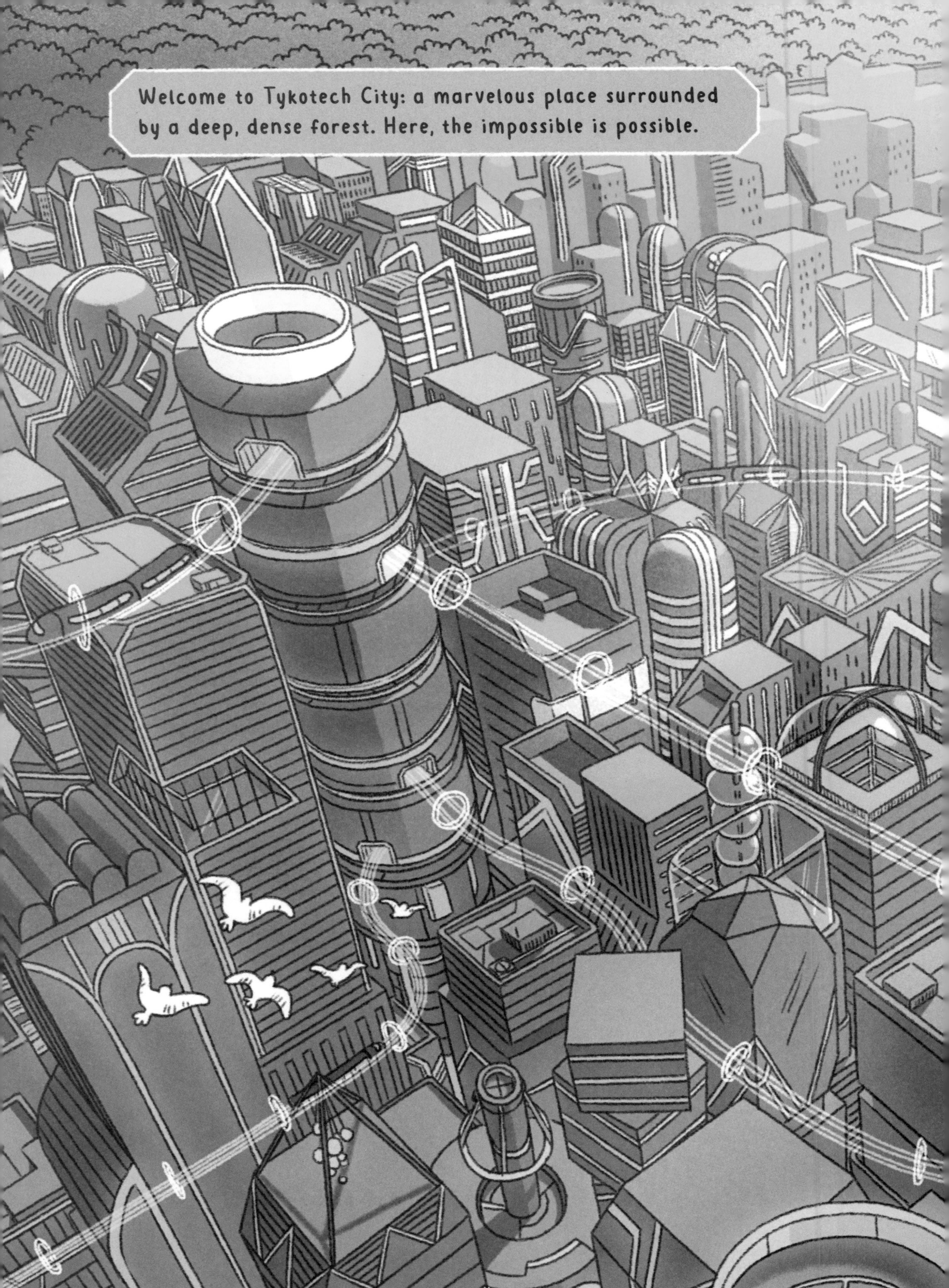
Welcome to Tykotech City: a marvelous place surrounded by a deep, dense forest. Here, the impossible is possible.

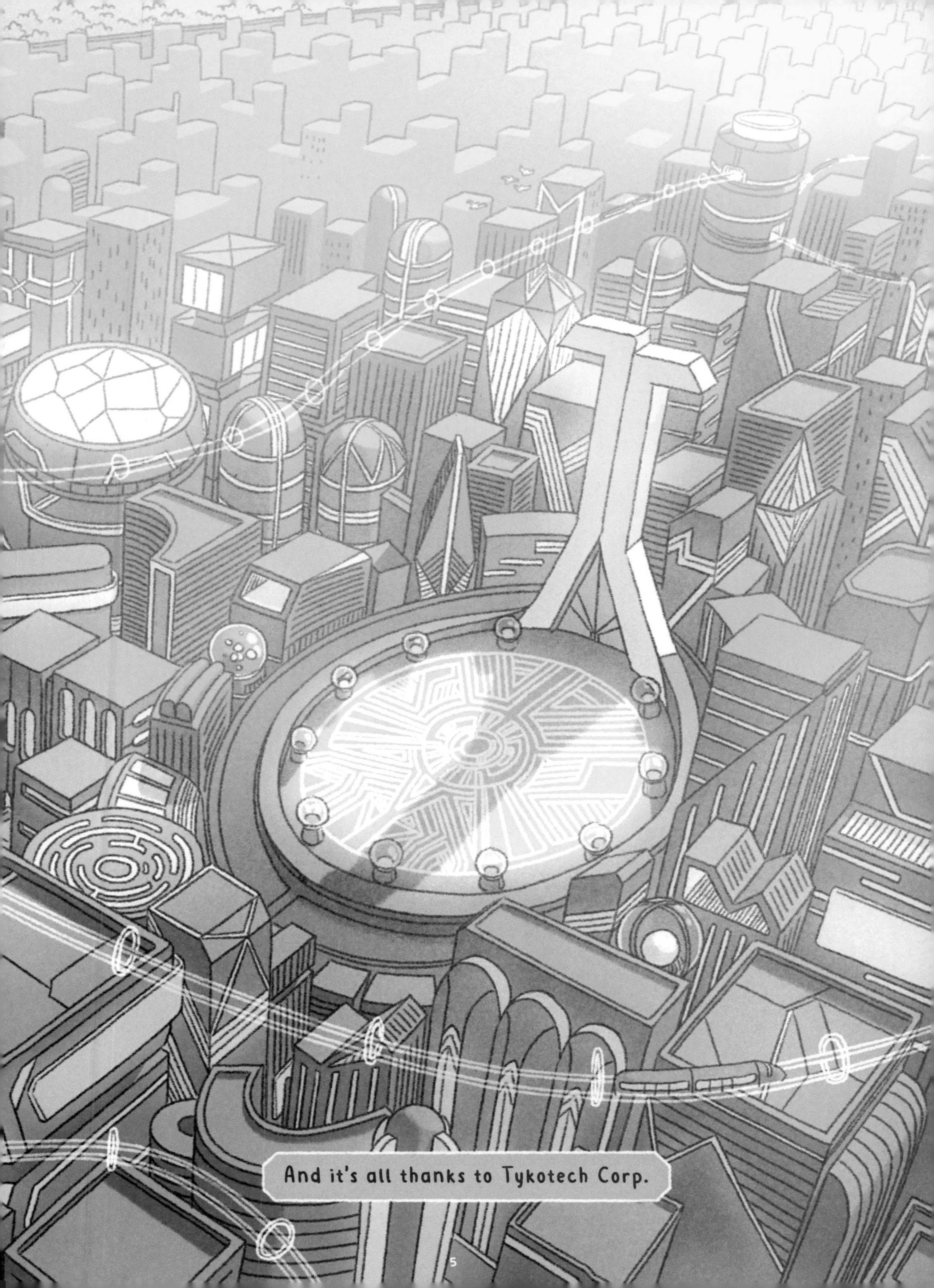
And it's all thanks to Tykotech Corp.

Many years ago, Tykotech Corp invented The Core: an energy source to power the whole city wirelessly. Never again would the cityfolk need to wander into the dangerous forest for resources.

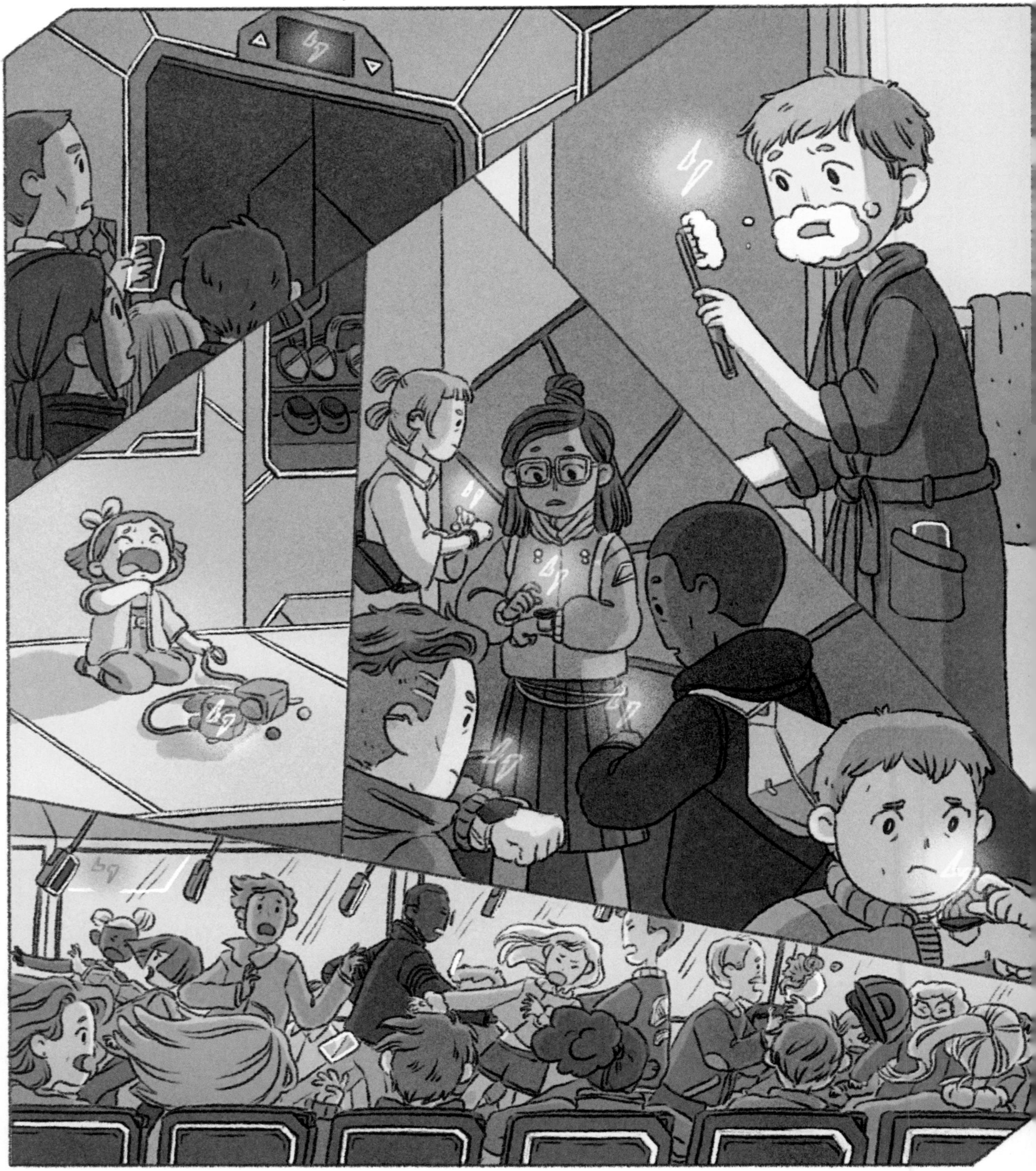

But now, something was horribly wrong with The Core.

Tykotech Corp scientists raced to find a solution to the power cuts, before the city was plunged into darkness. But nothing seemed to be working.

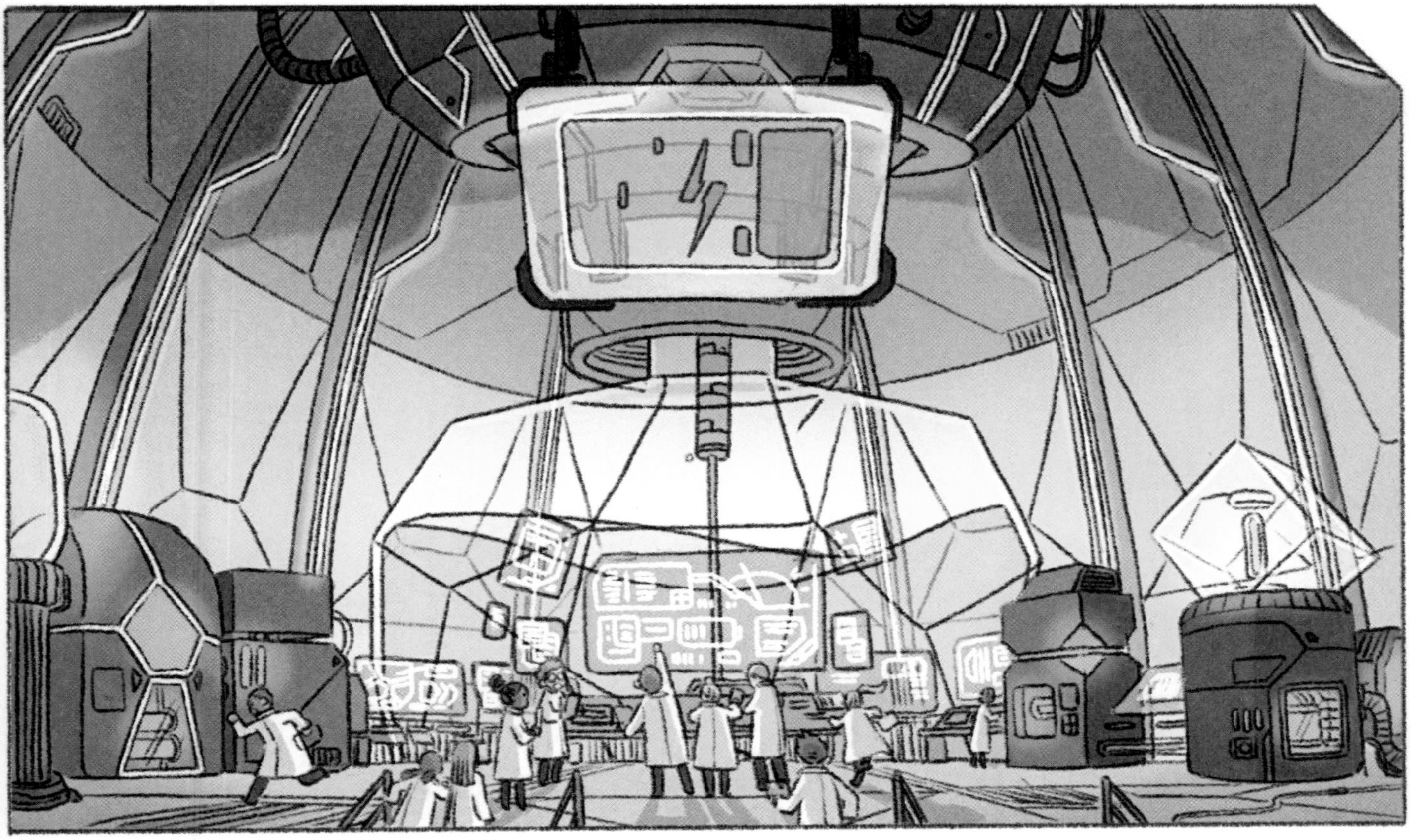

President Kozen, the head of Tykotech Corp, wanted them to expand their search to the forest. But dangerous beasts were said to roam there, and no one had ventured beyond the walls for as long as anyone could remember.

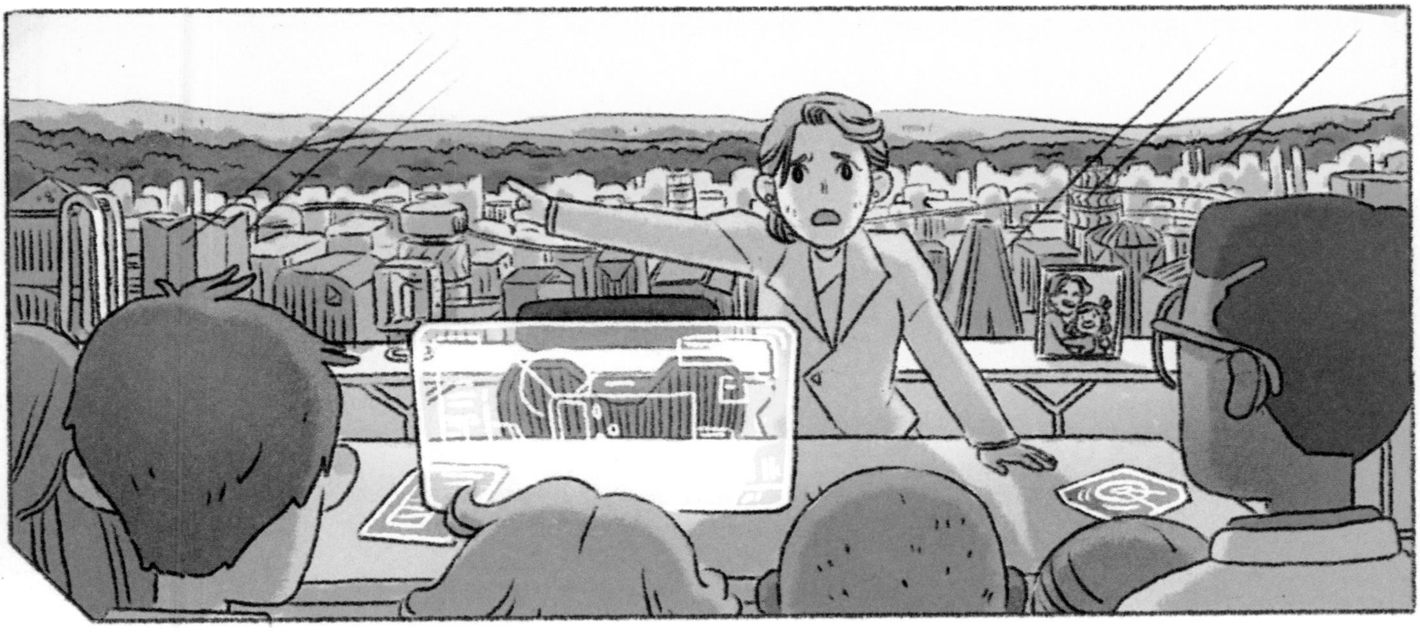

Little did they know that the solution to their problems lay in the hands of a small girl. One who tinkered away in her room all day, using spare parts from her dad's repair shop to invent all sorts of useful things...

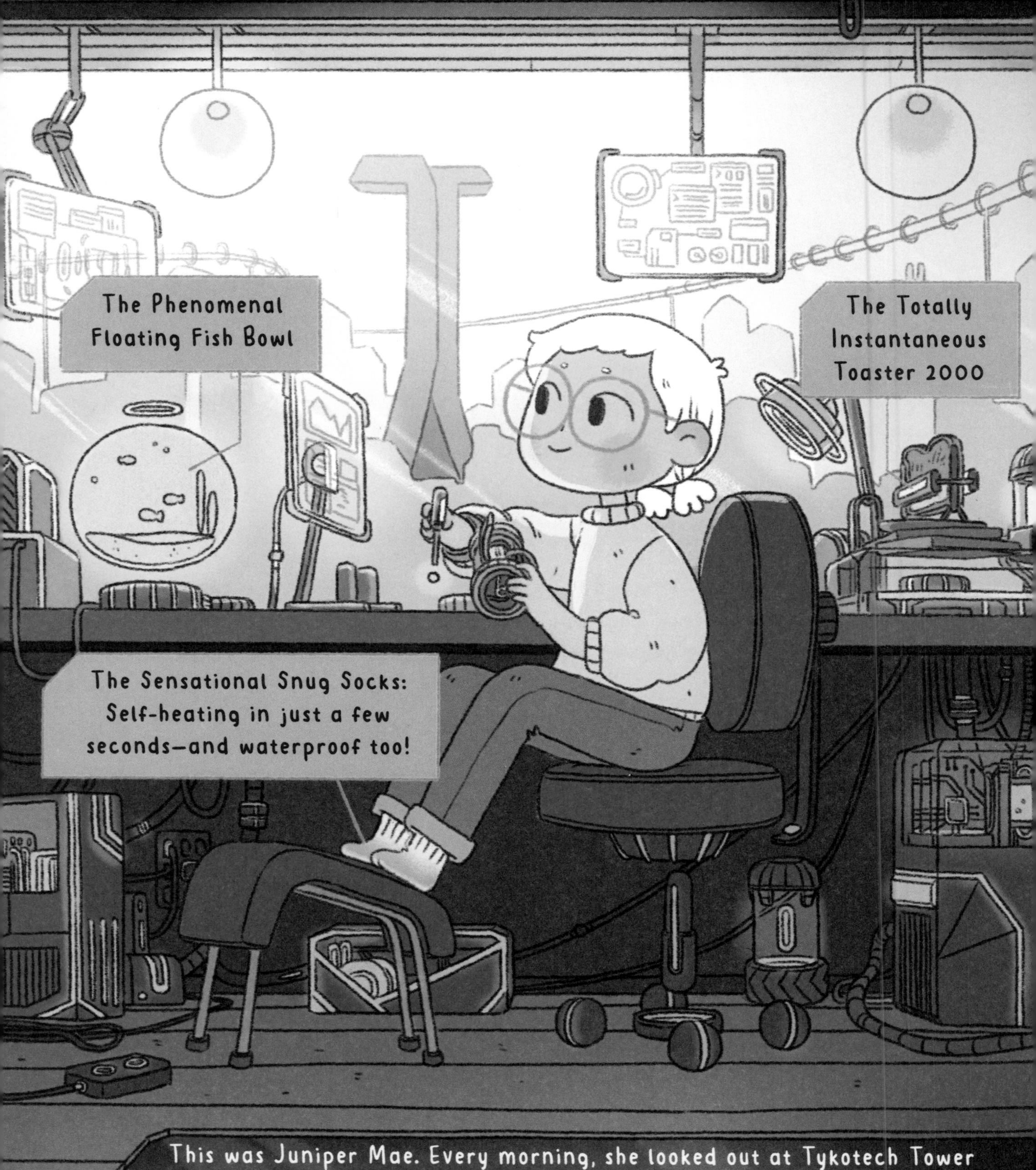
The Phenomenal Floating Fish Bowl
The Totally Instantaneous Toaster 2000
The Sensational Snug Socks: Self-heating in just a few seconds—and waterproof too!

This was Juniper Mae. Every morning, she looked out at Tykotech Tower from her window, dreaming of one day working there as a great inventor.

And when she wasn't inventing, she was reading her favorite fables about legendary warriors who protected the city from danger.

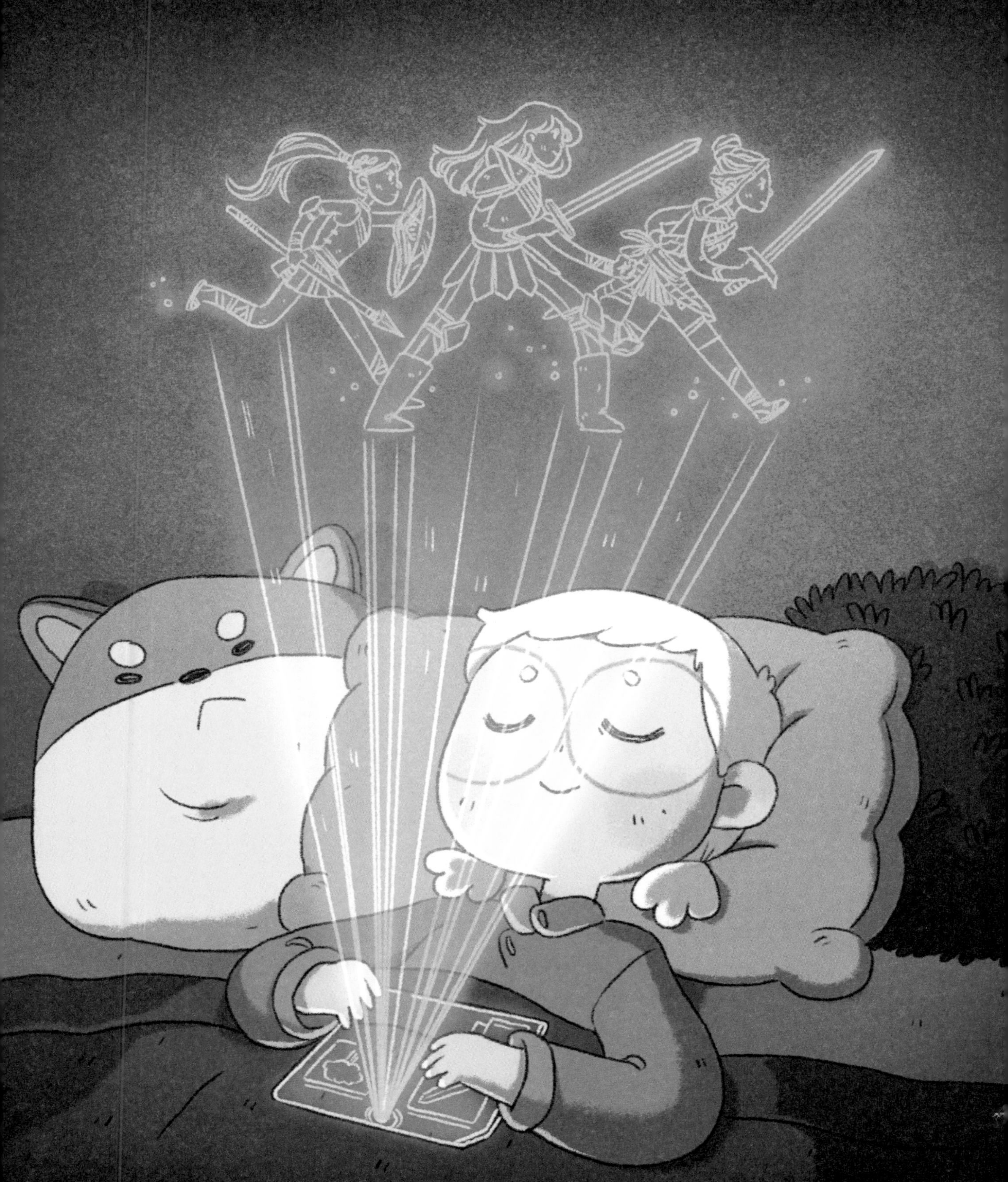

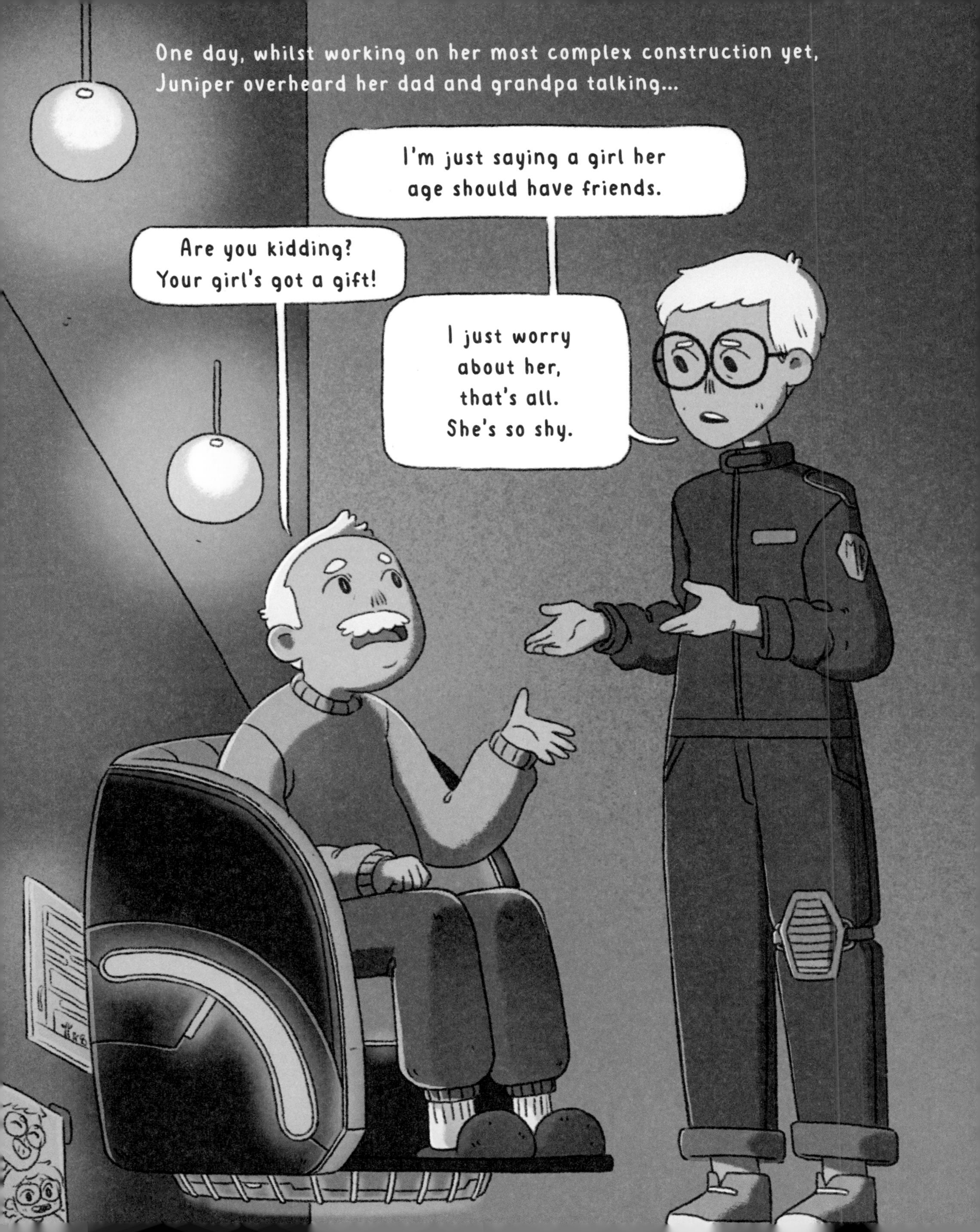
One day, whilst working on her most complex construction yet, Juniper overheard her dad and grandpa talking...
I'm just saying a girl her age should have friends.
Are you kidding? Your girl's got a gift!
I just worry about her, that's all. She's so shy.

In her fables, the mightiest heroes all relied on each other. But Juniper told herself that she didn't need friends. Her creations were enough.

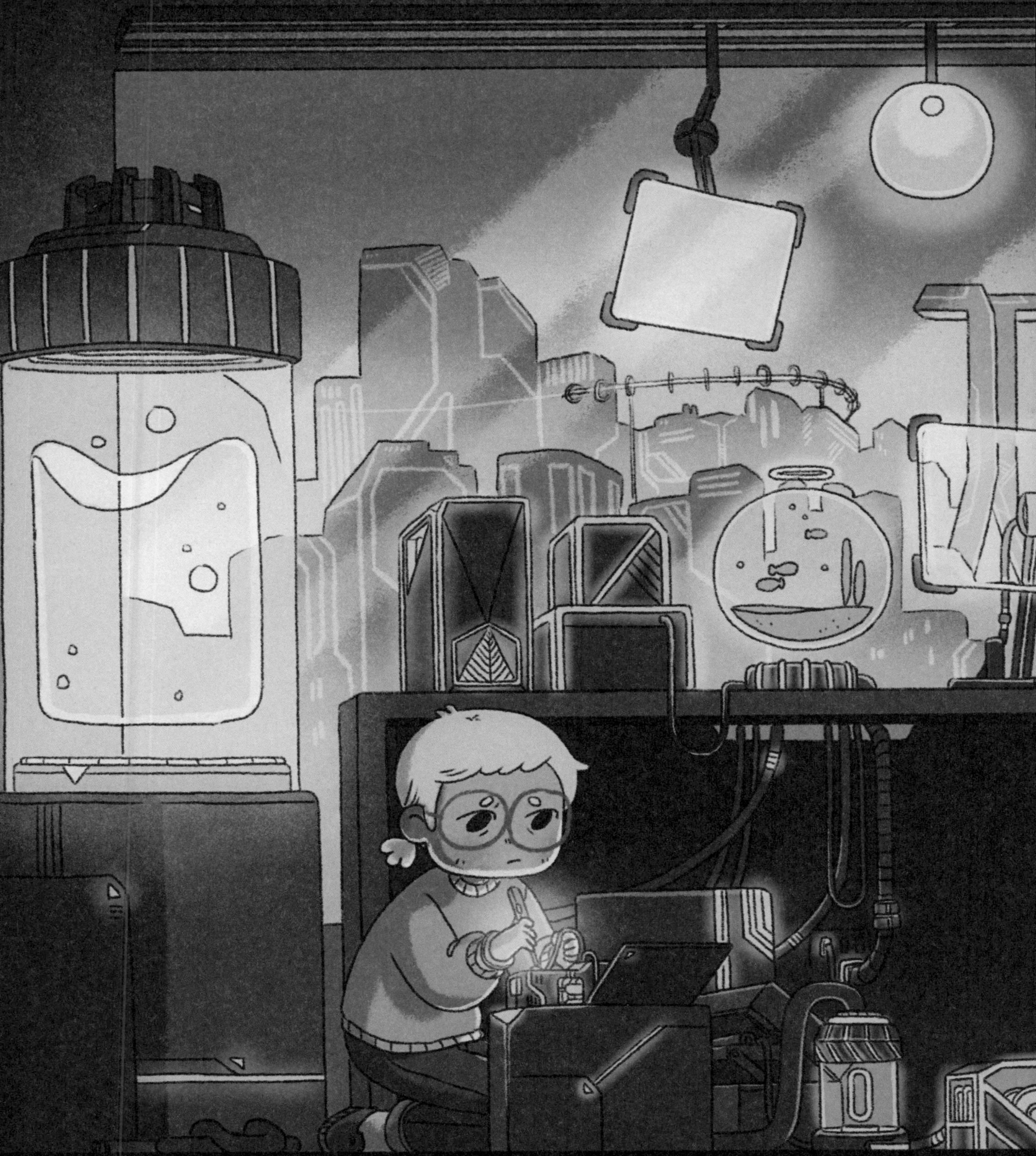

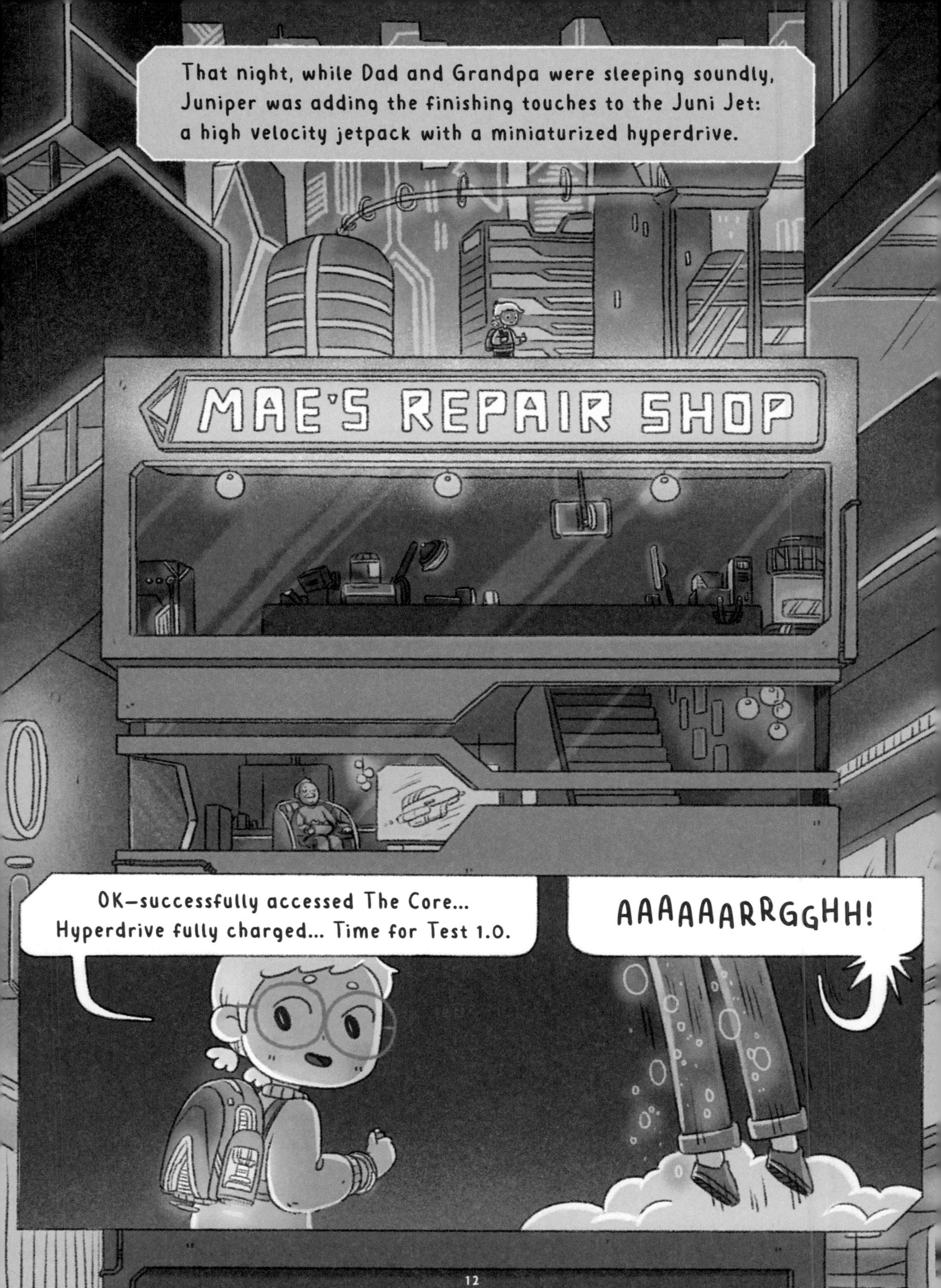

That night, while Dad and Grandpa were sleeping soundly, Juniper was adding the finishing touches to the Juni Jet: a high velocity jetpack with a miniaturized hyperdrive.
MAE'S REPAIR SHOP
OK—successfully accessed The Core... Hyperdrive fully charged... Time for Test 1.0.
AAAAAARRGGHH!

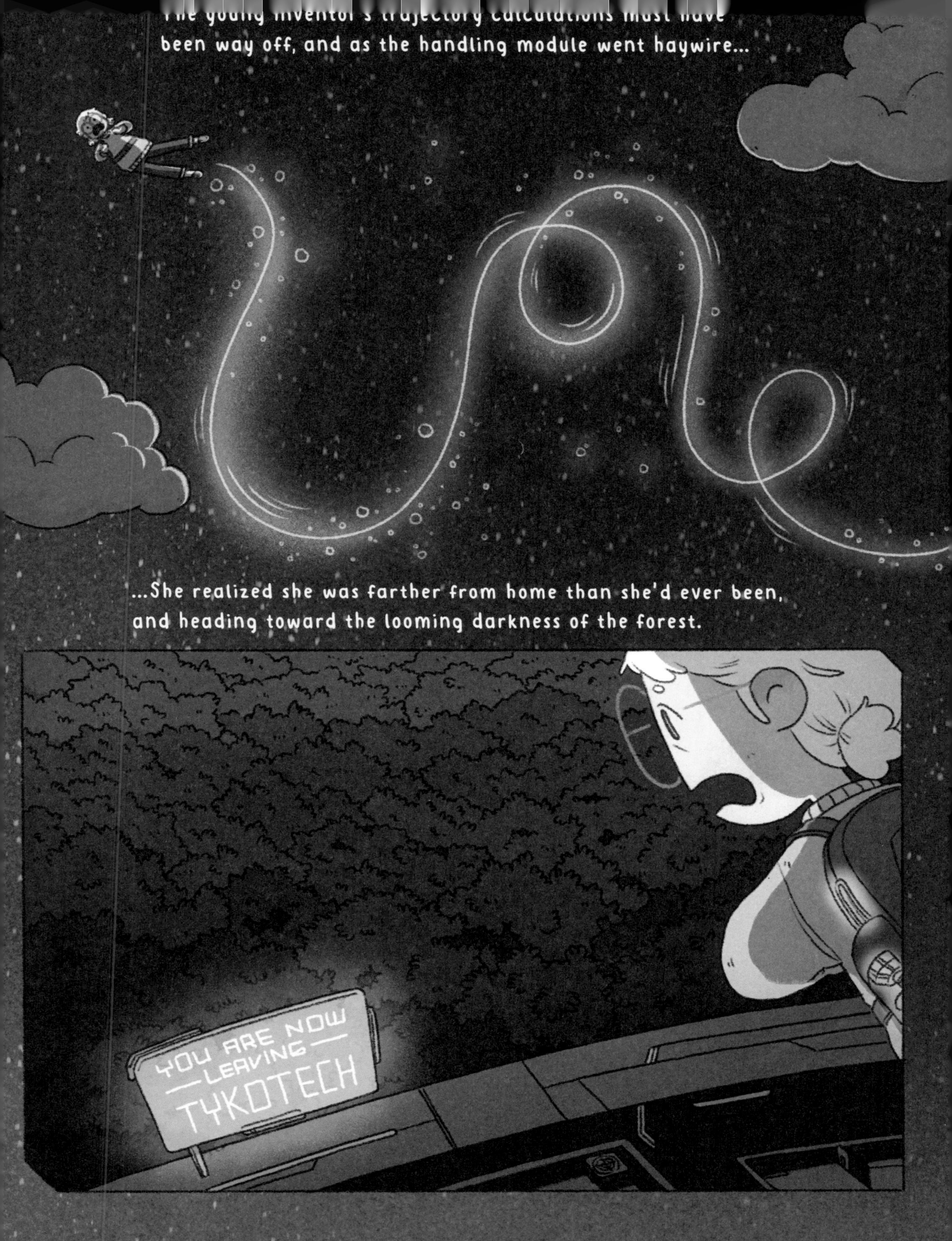
The young inventor's trajectory calculations must have been way off, and as the handling module went haywire...
...She realized she was farther from home than she'd ever been, and heading toward the looming darkness of the forest.
YOU ARE NOW
LEAVING
TYKOTECH

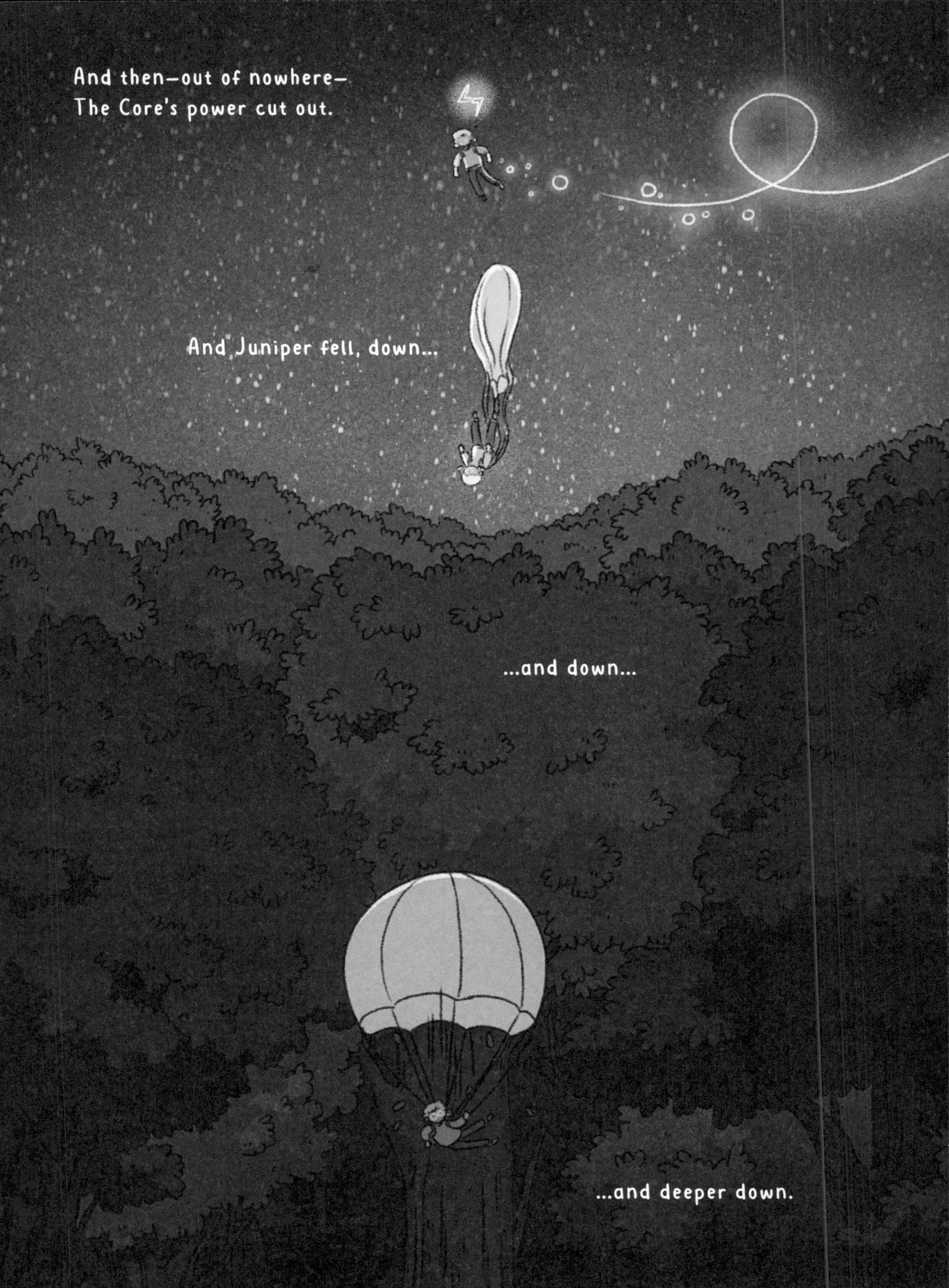
And then—out of nowhere—
The Core's power cut out.
And Juniper fell, down...
...and down...
...and deeper down.

Juniper shivered as she looked around the spooky trees. How was she going to get home? The Juni Jet was busted beyond repair and she was very lost and—

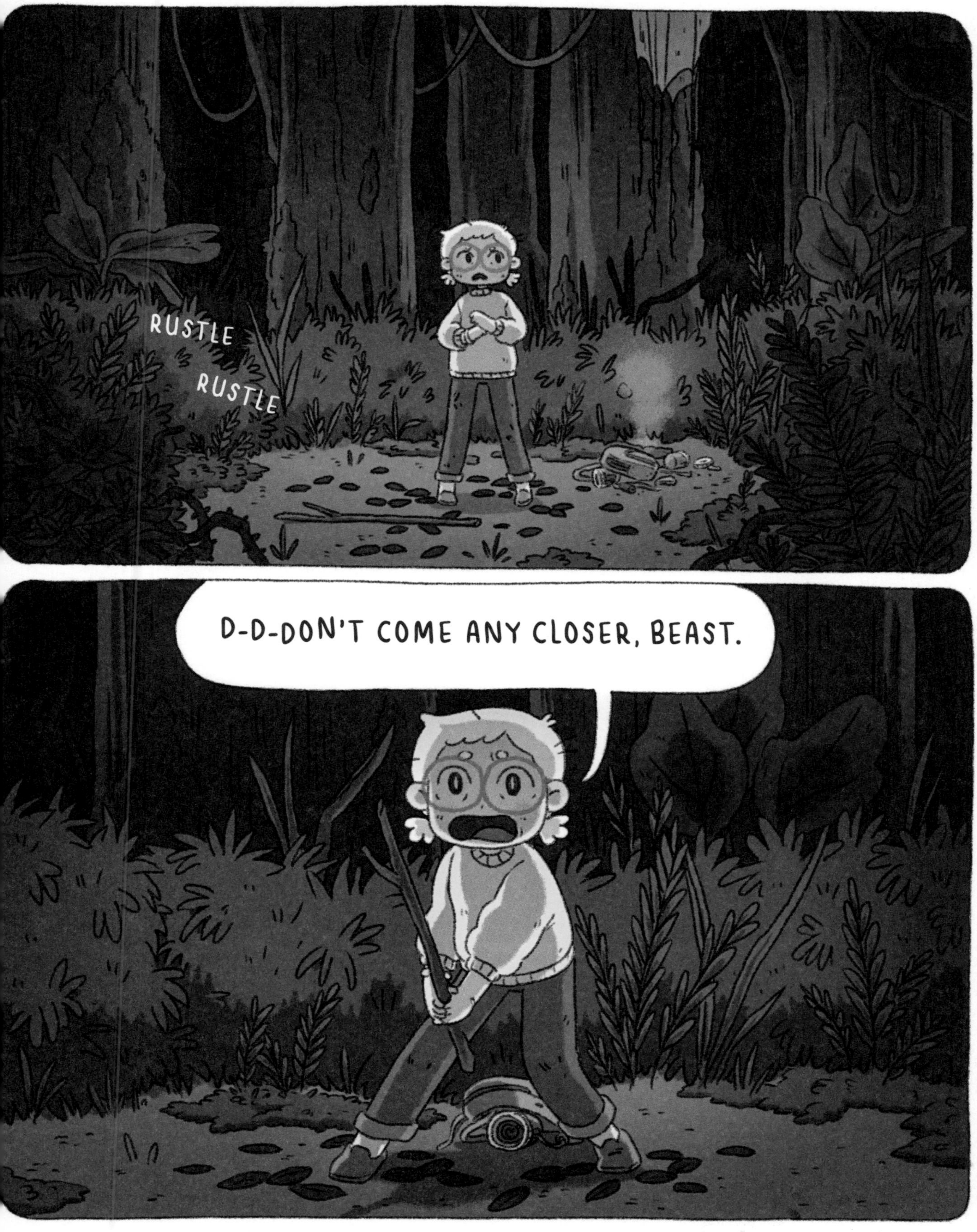
RUSTLE
RUSTLE
D-D-DON'T COME ANY CLOSER, BEAST.

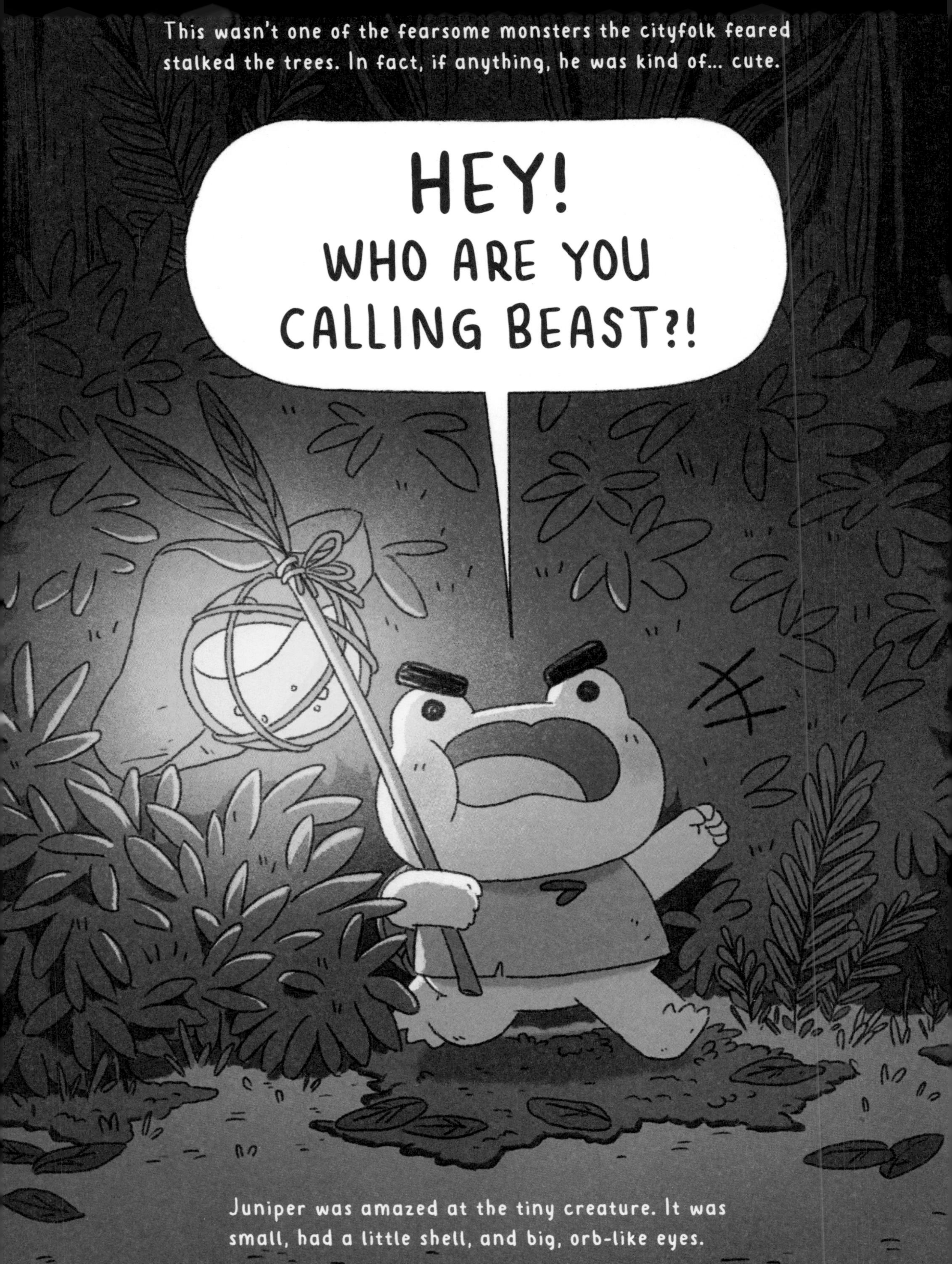
This wasn't one of the fearsome monsters the cityfolk feared stalked the trees. In fact, if anything, he was kind of... cute.
HEY! WHO ARE YOU CALLING BEAST?!
Juniper was amazed at the tiny creature. It was small, had a little shell, and big, orb-like eyes.

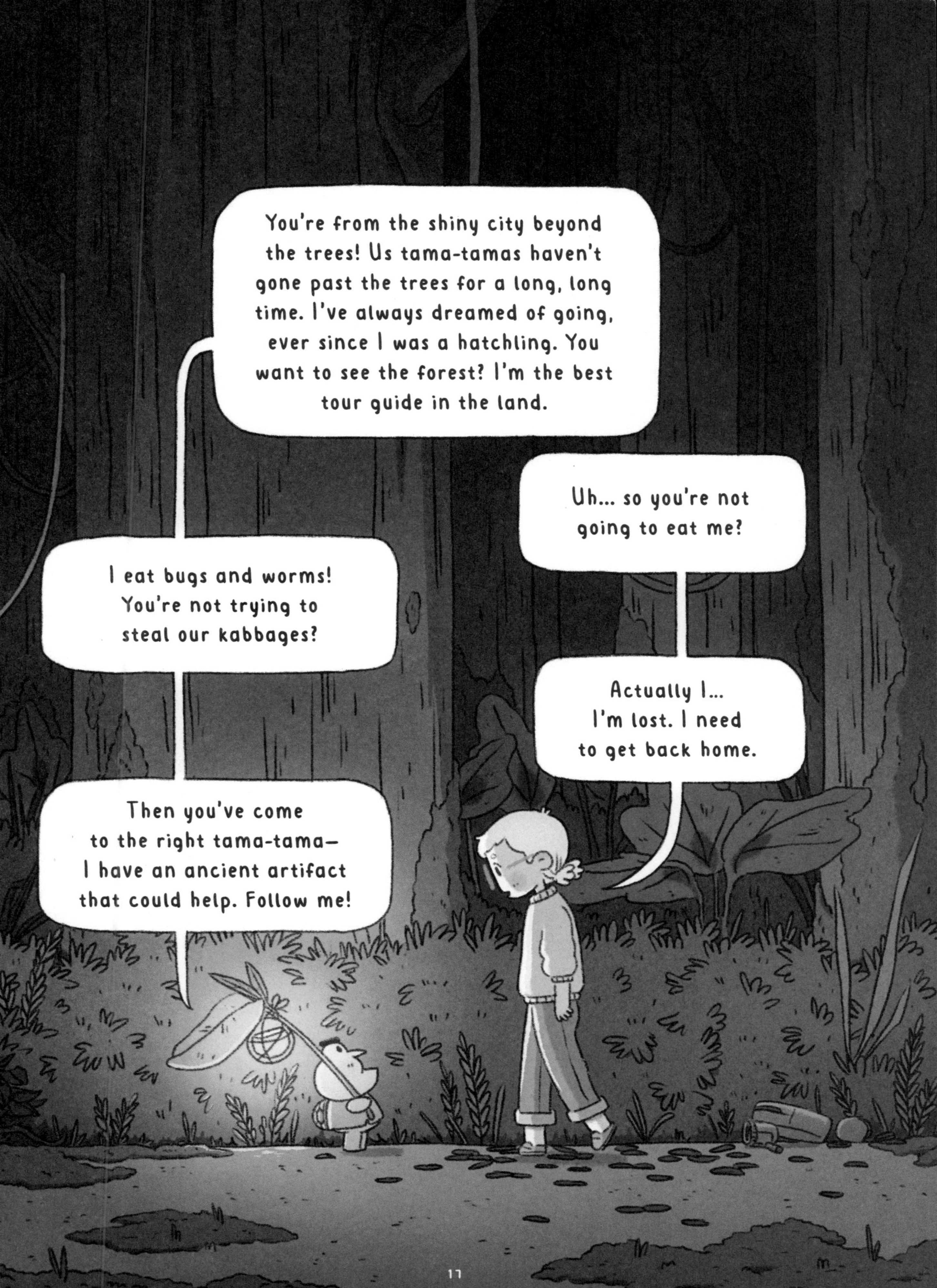
You're from the shiny city beyond the trees! Us tama-tamas haven't gone past the trees for a long, long time. I've always dreamed of going, ever since I was a hatchling. You want to see the forest? I'm the best tour guide in the land.
Uh... so you're not going to eat me?
I eat bugs and worms! You're not trying to steal our kabbages?
Actually I... I'm lost. I need to get back home.
Then you've come to the right tama-tama— I have an ancient artifact that could help. Follow me!

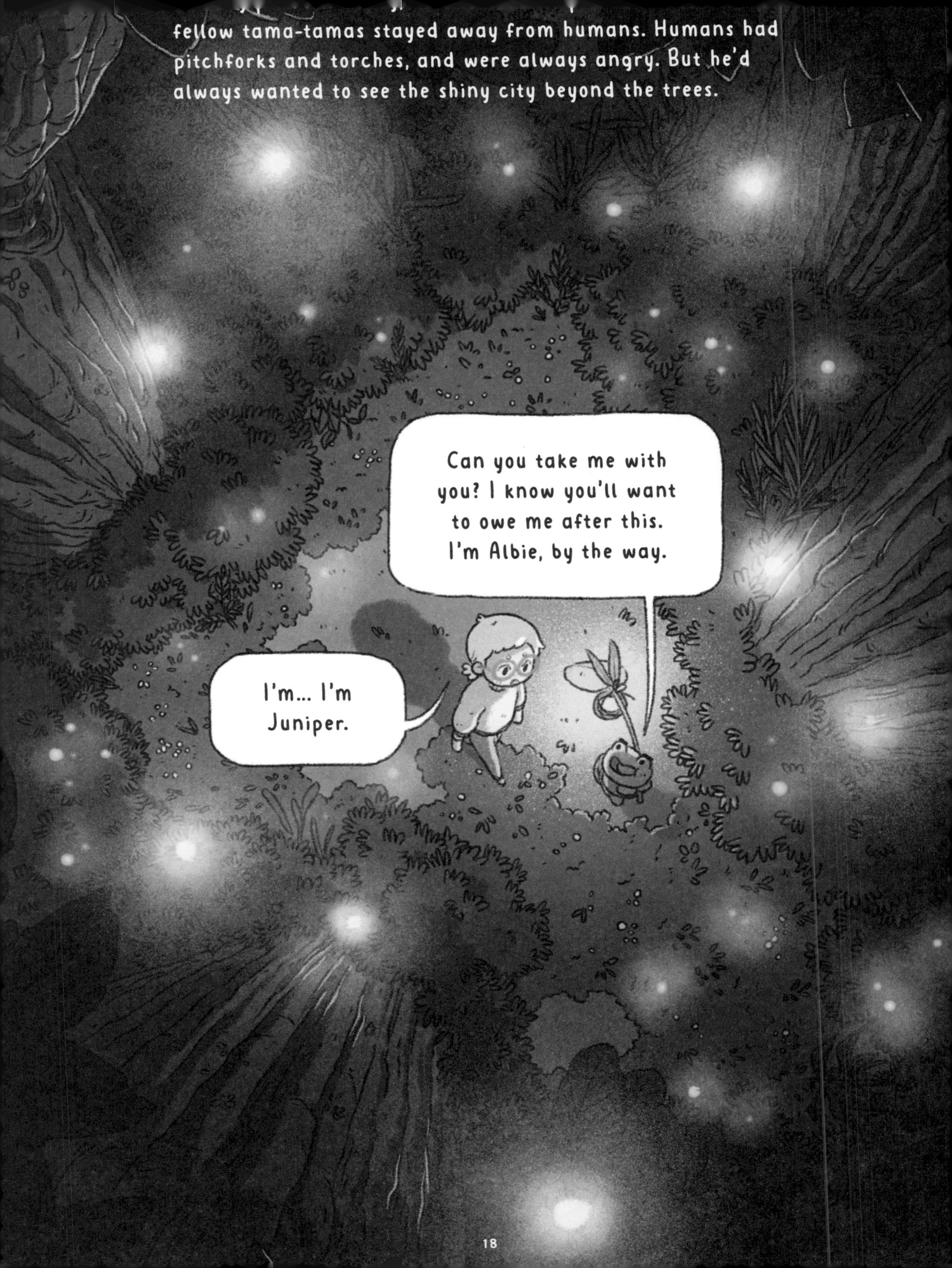
fellow tama-tamas stayed away from humans. Humans had pitchforks and torches, and were always angry. But he'd always wanted to see the shiny city beyond the trees.
Can you take me with you? I know you'll want to owe me after this. I'm Albie, by the way.
I'm... I'm Juniper.

Albie did indeed know the forest very well.
He steered Juniper clear of the hugging vines and sinking mud...

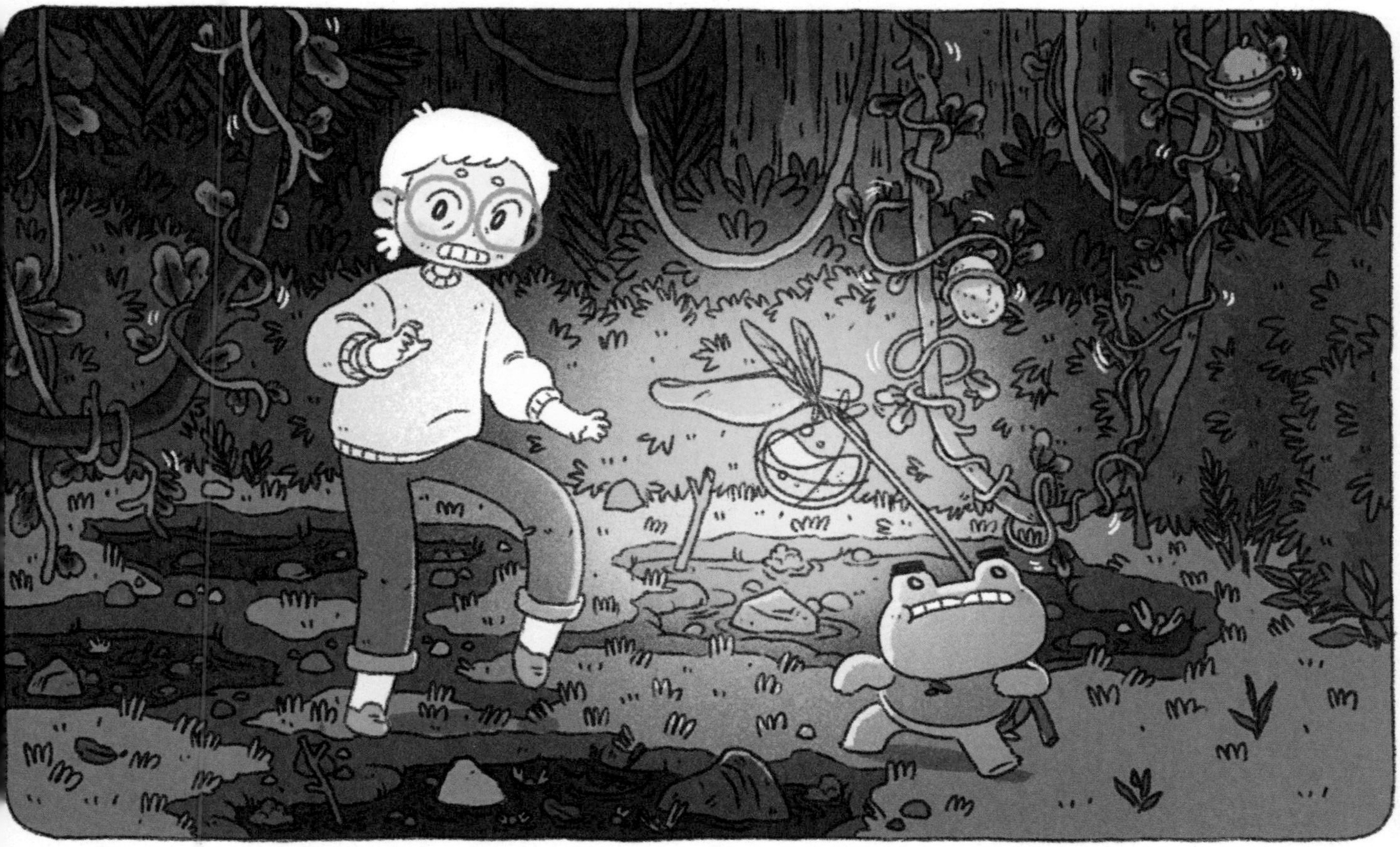

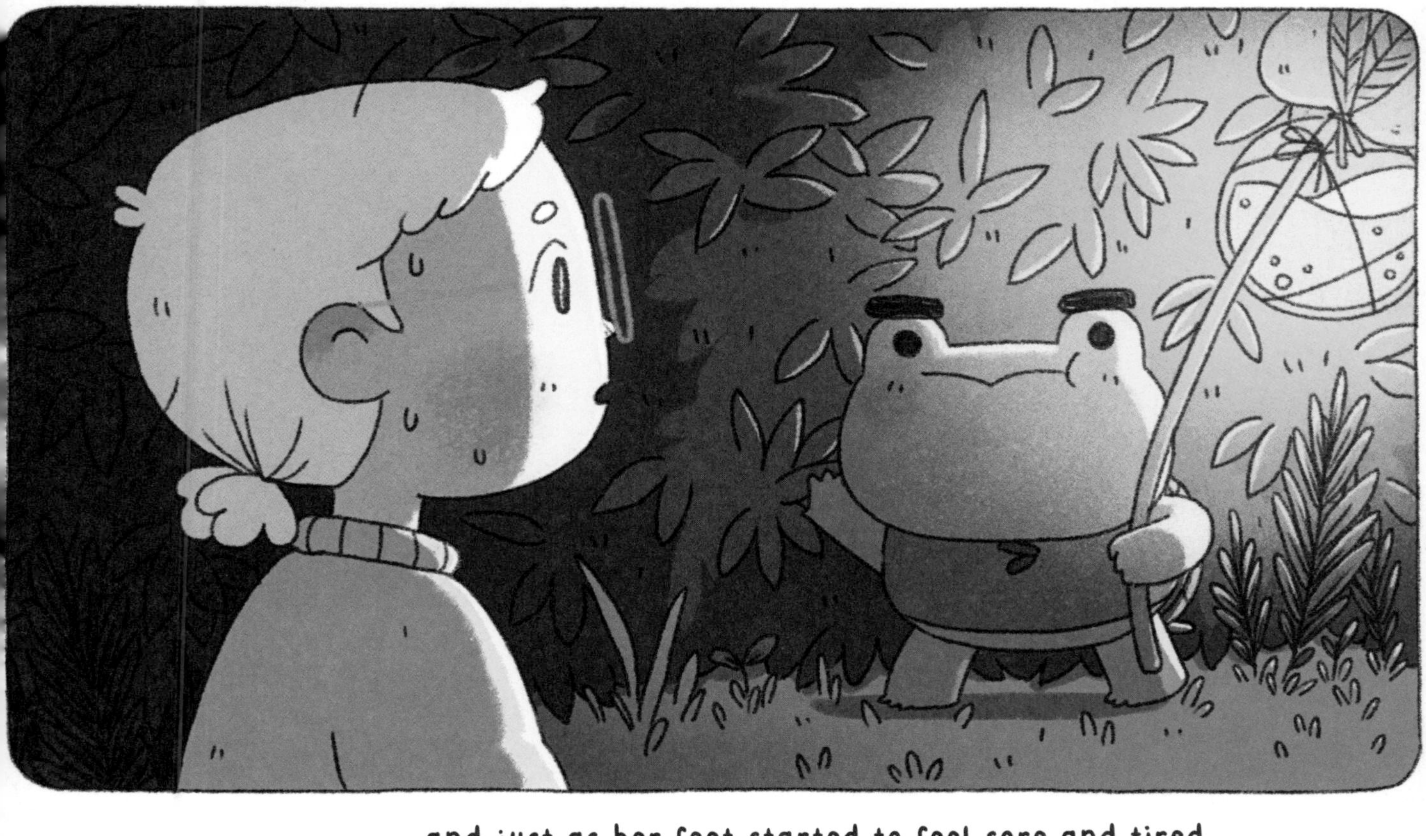

...and just as her feet started to feel sore and tired,
Juniper noticed a warm orange glow emerging from the foliage...

Albie parted the bushes to reveal a whole village filled with tama-tamas, young and old. And not a beast in sight!

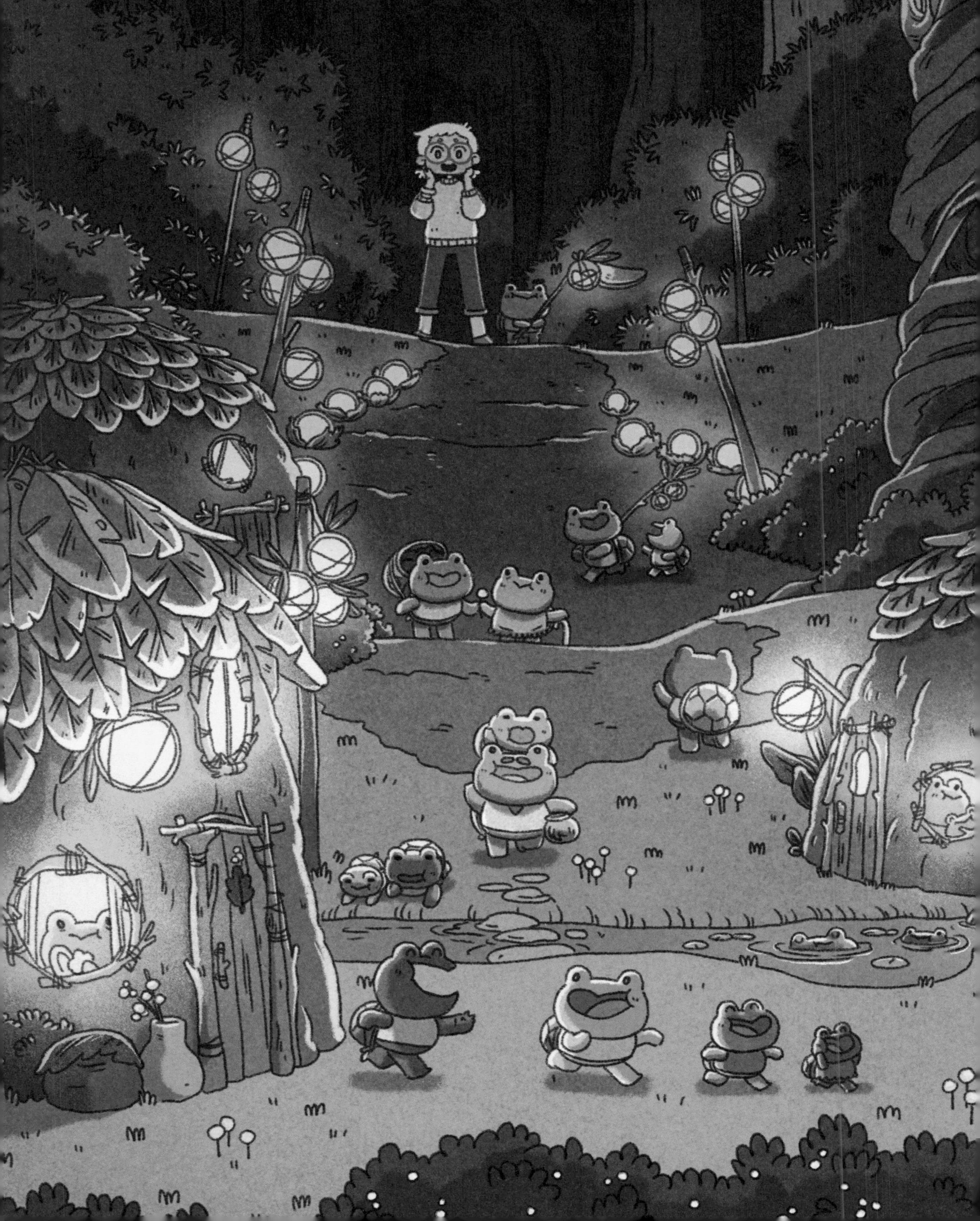

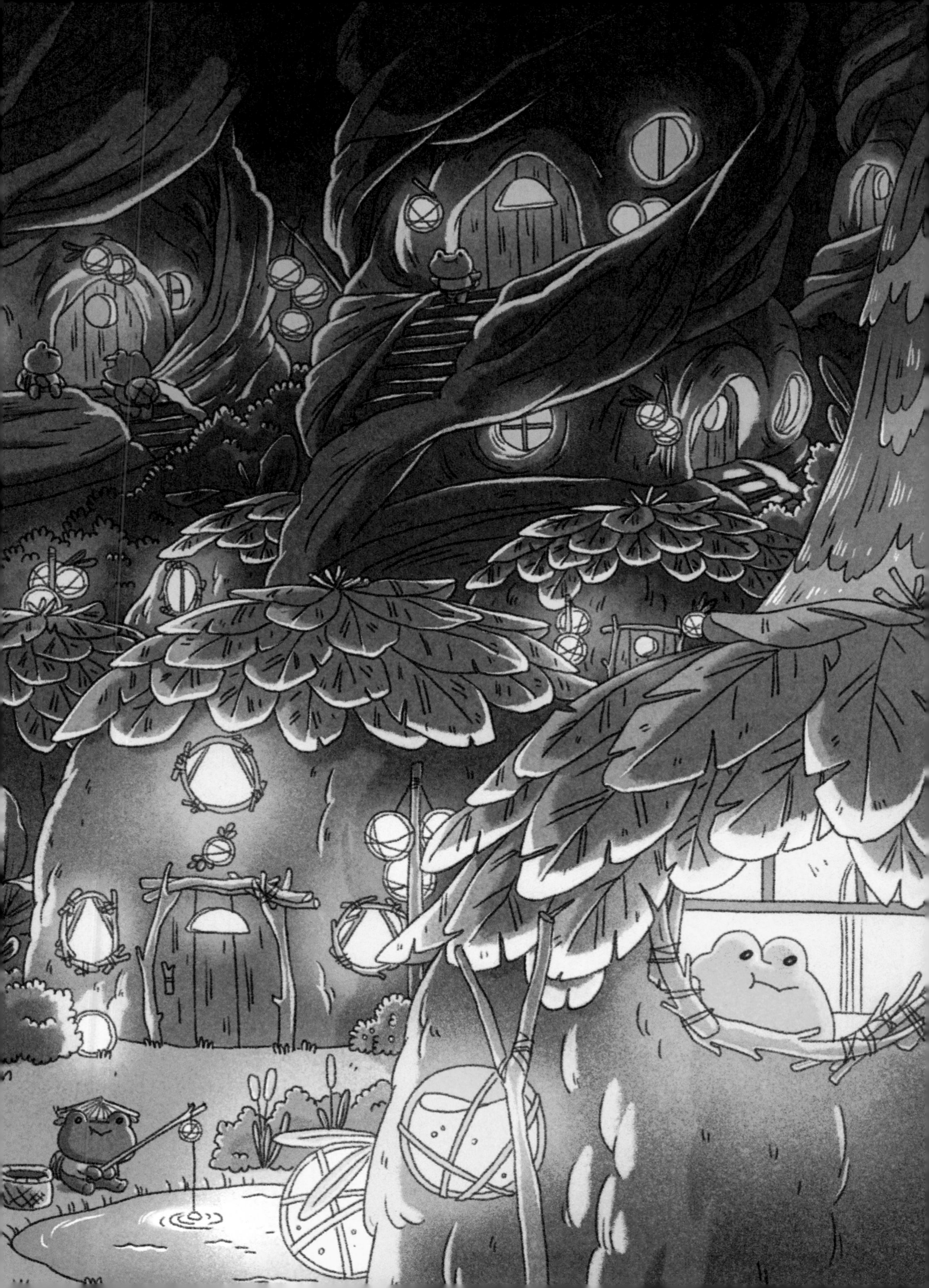

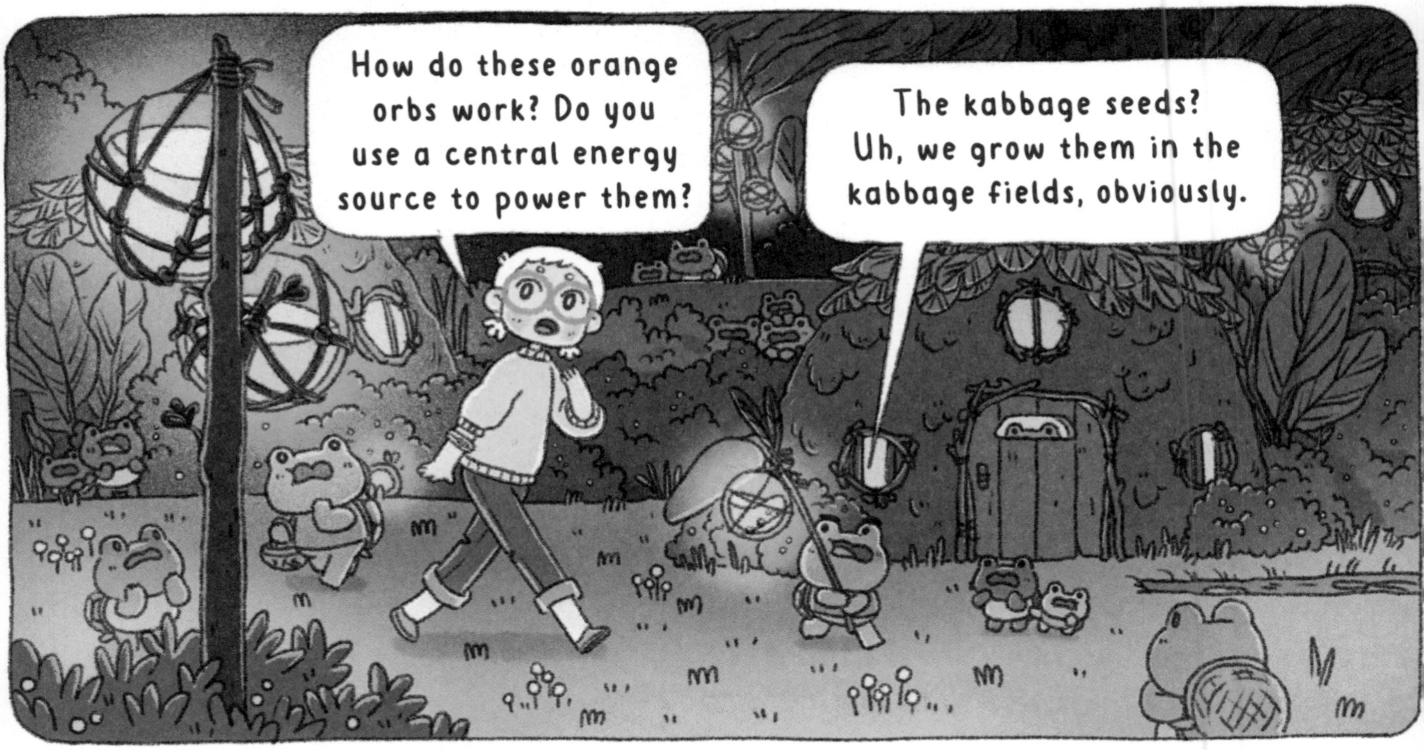
How do these orange orbs work? Do you use a central energy source to power them?
The kabbage seeds? Uh, we grow them in the kabbage fields, obviously.

Albie led a wide-eyed Juniper past the staring tama-tamas to his hut. There he showed her the artifact that he'd been talking about...

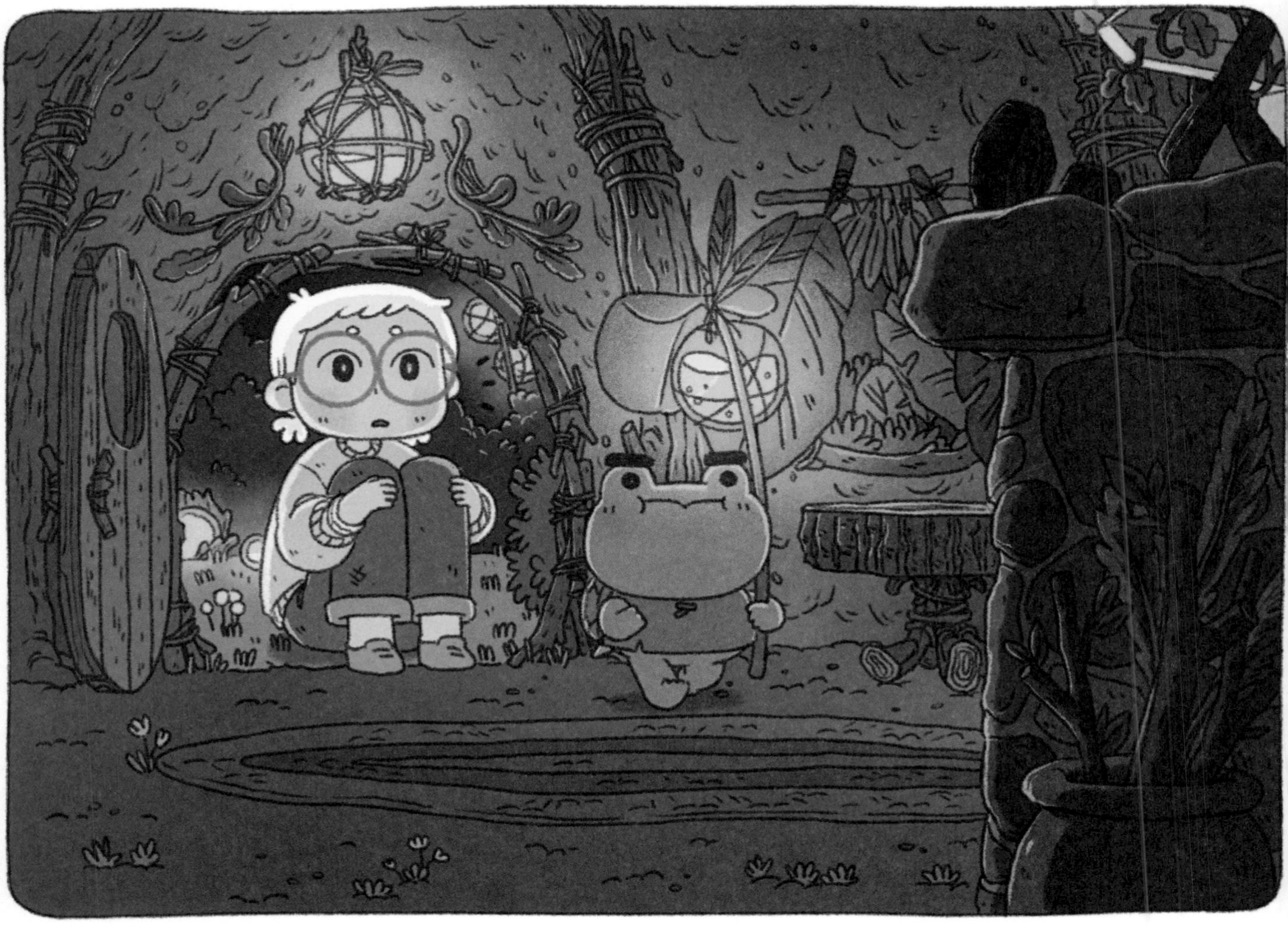

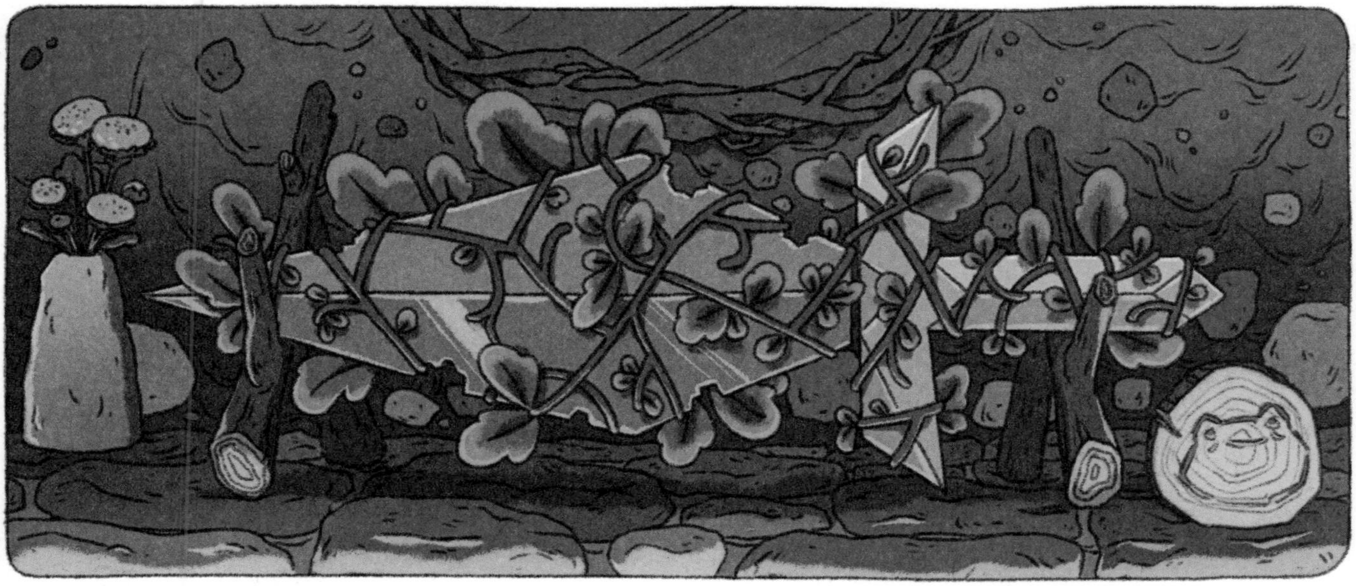

It looked just like something a warrior would wield in one of her fables!
Albie explained that it was a greatsword, used by the Guardian Knights eons ago.

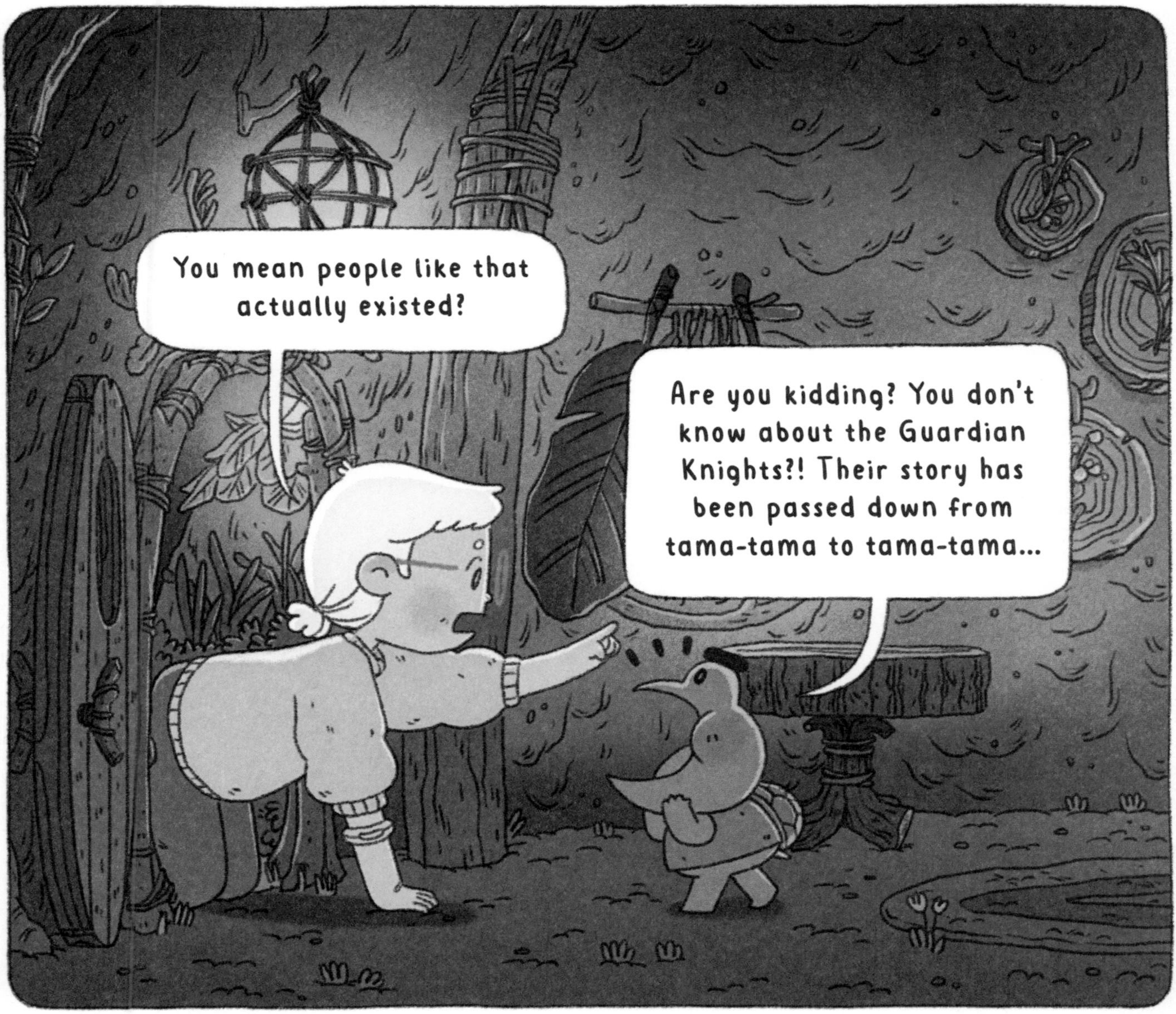
You mean people like that actually existed?
Are you kidding? You don't know about the Guardian Knights?! Their story has been passed down from tama-tama to tama-tama...

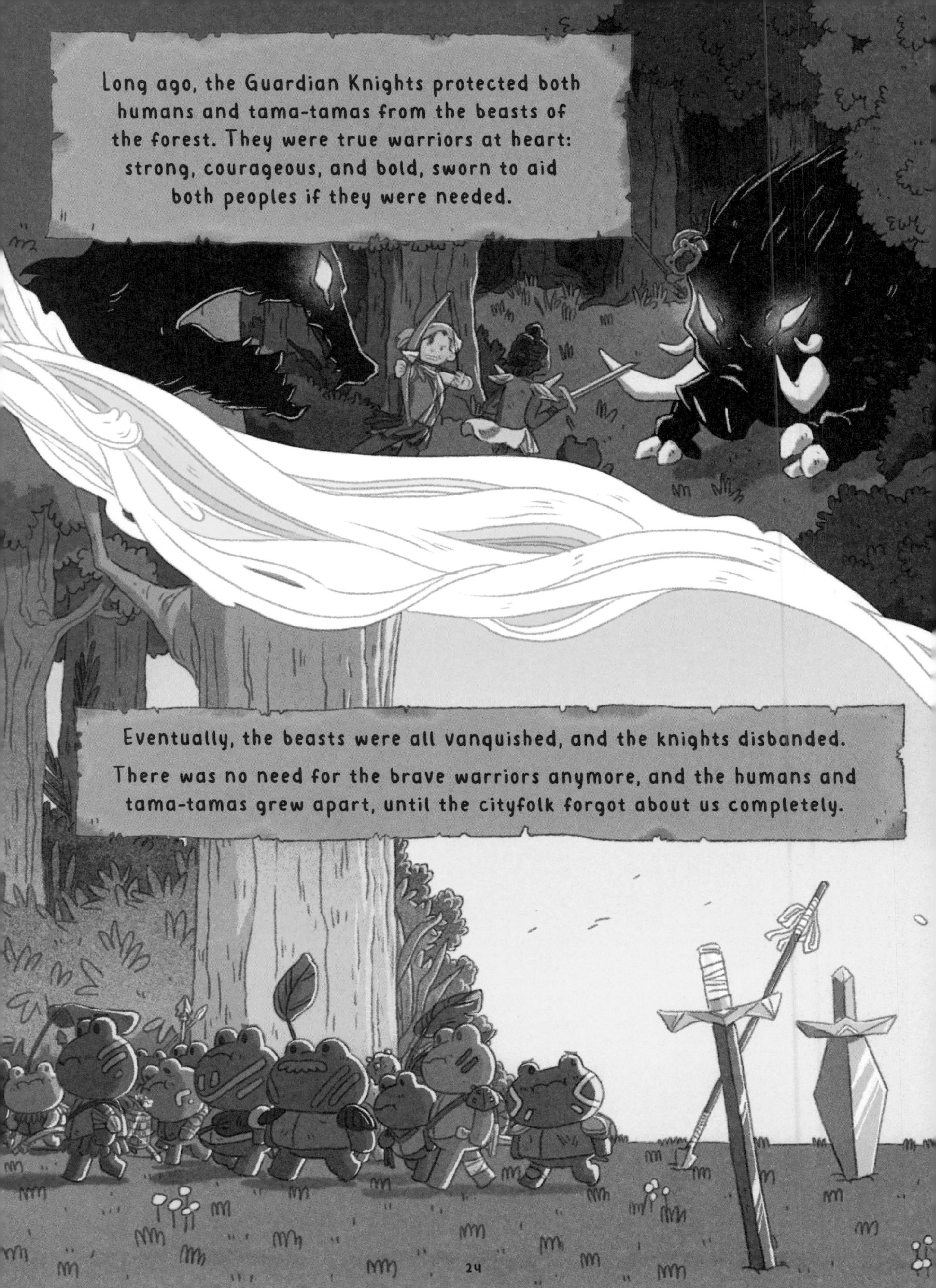
Long ago, the Guardian Knights protected both humans and tama-tamas from the beasts of the forest. They were true warriors at heart: strong, courageous, and bold, sworn to aid both peoples if they were needed.
Eventually, the beasts were all vanquished, and the knights disbanded.
There was no need for the brave warriors anymore, and the humans and tama-tamas grew apart, until the cityfolk forgot about us completely.

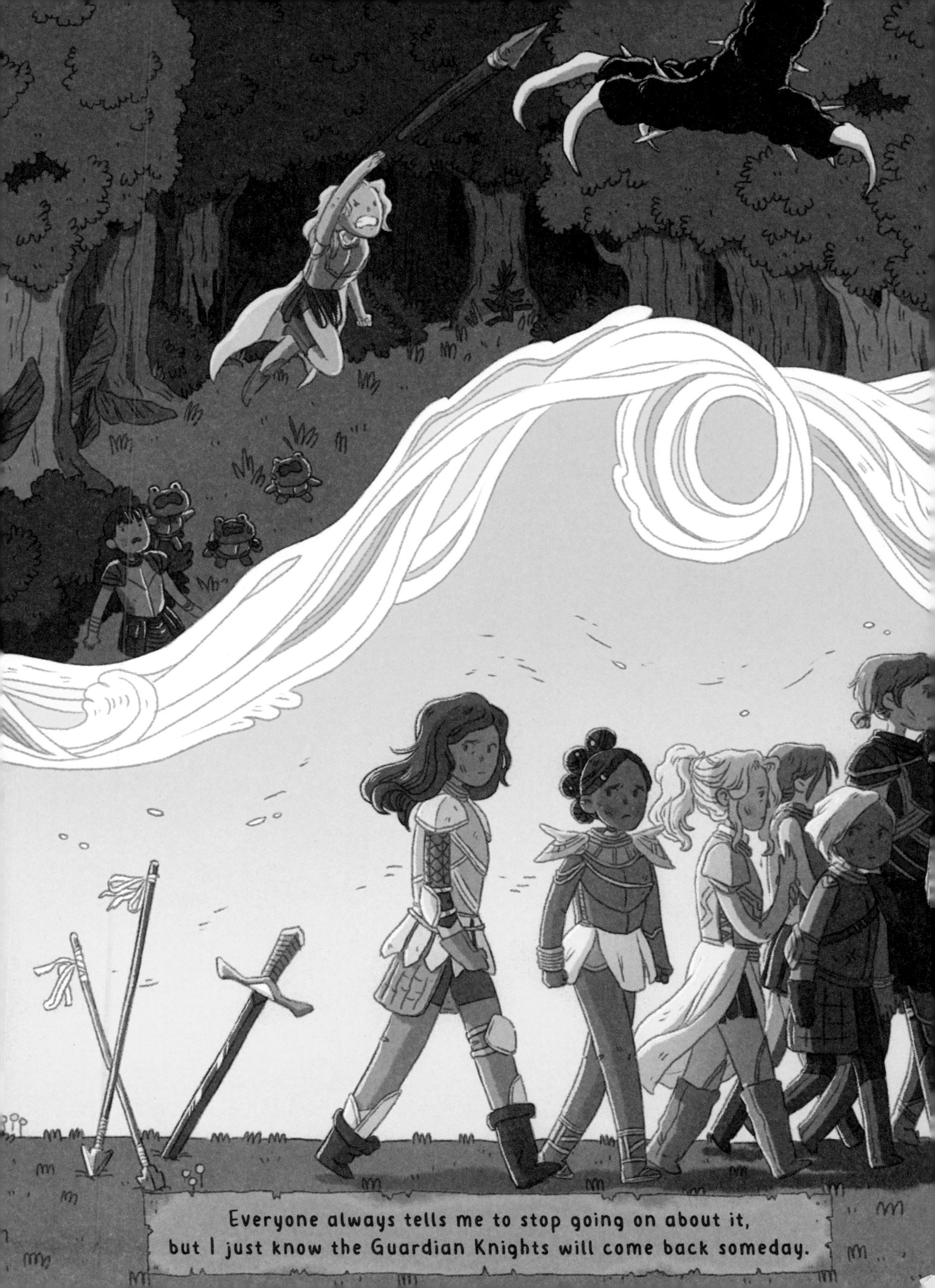
Everyone always tells me to stop going on about it,
but I just know the Guardian Knights will come back someday.

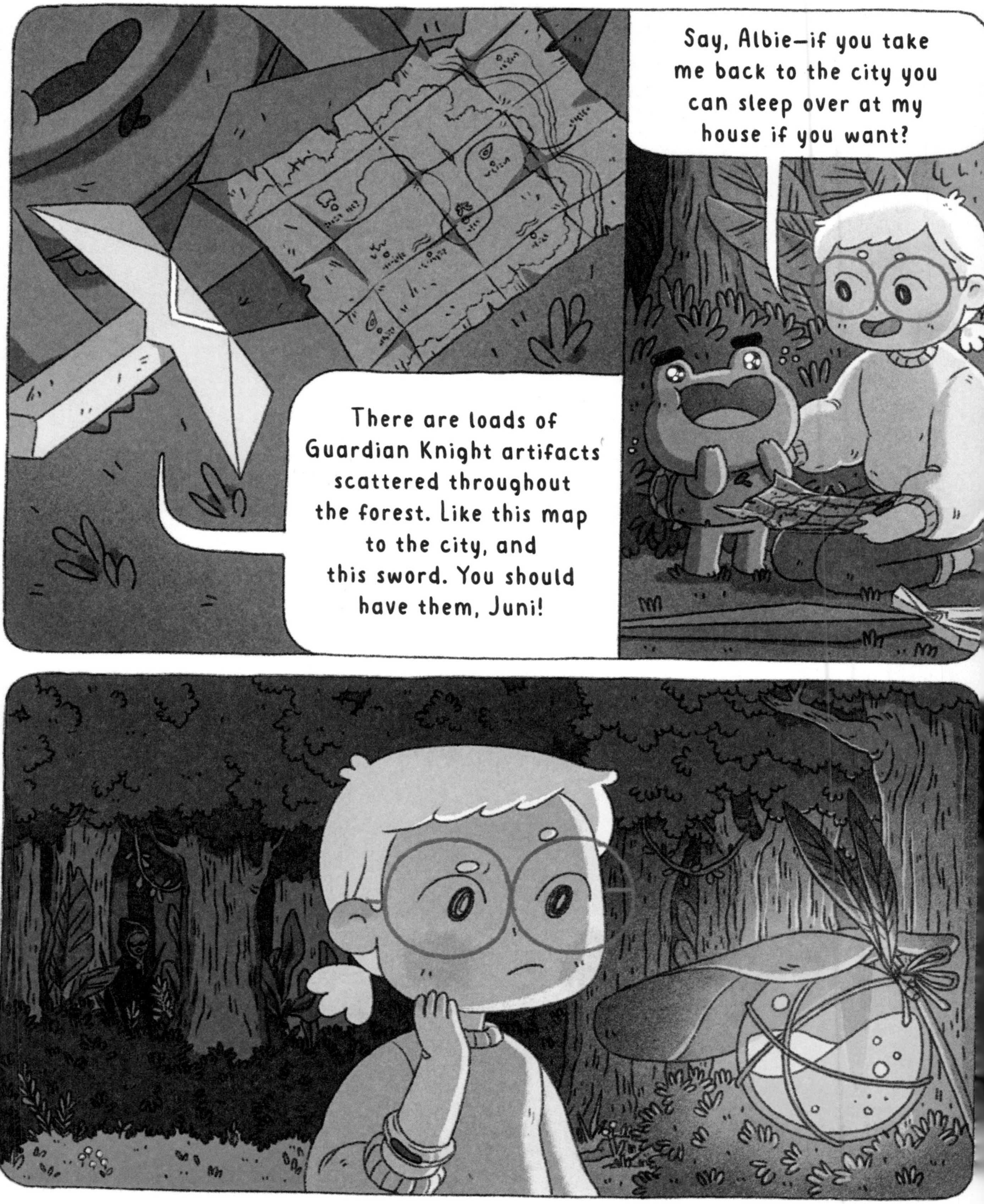
There are loads of Guardian Knight artifacts scattered throughout the forest. Like this map to the city, and this sword. You should have them, Juni!
Say, Albie—if you take me back to the city you can sleep over at my house if you want?

As they headed homeward, Juniper's mind raced with countless questions. Could the Guardian Knights really have existed? What made this mysterious kabbage seed glow?

oon enough, Albie led Juniper to the familiar lights of the city that she called home...

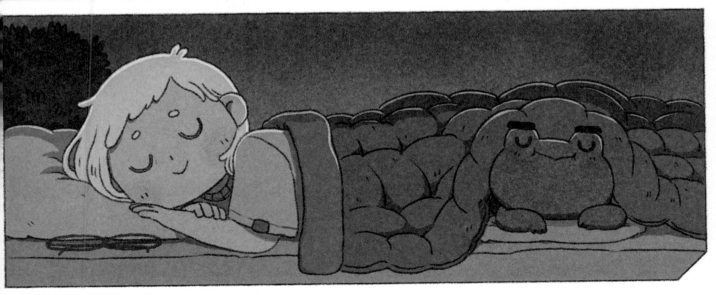

The next morning, Juniper was so excited she couldn't sit still.

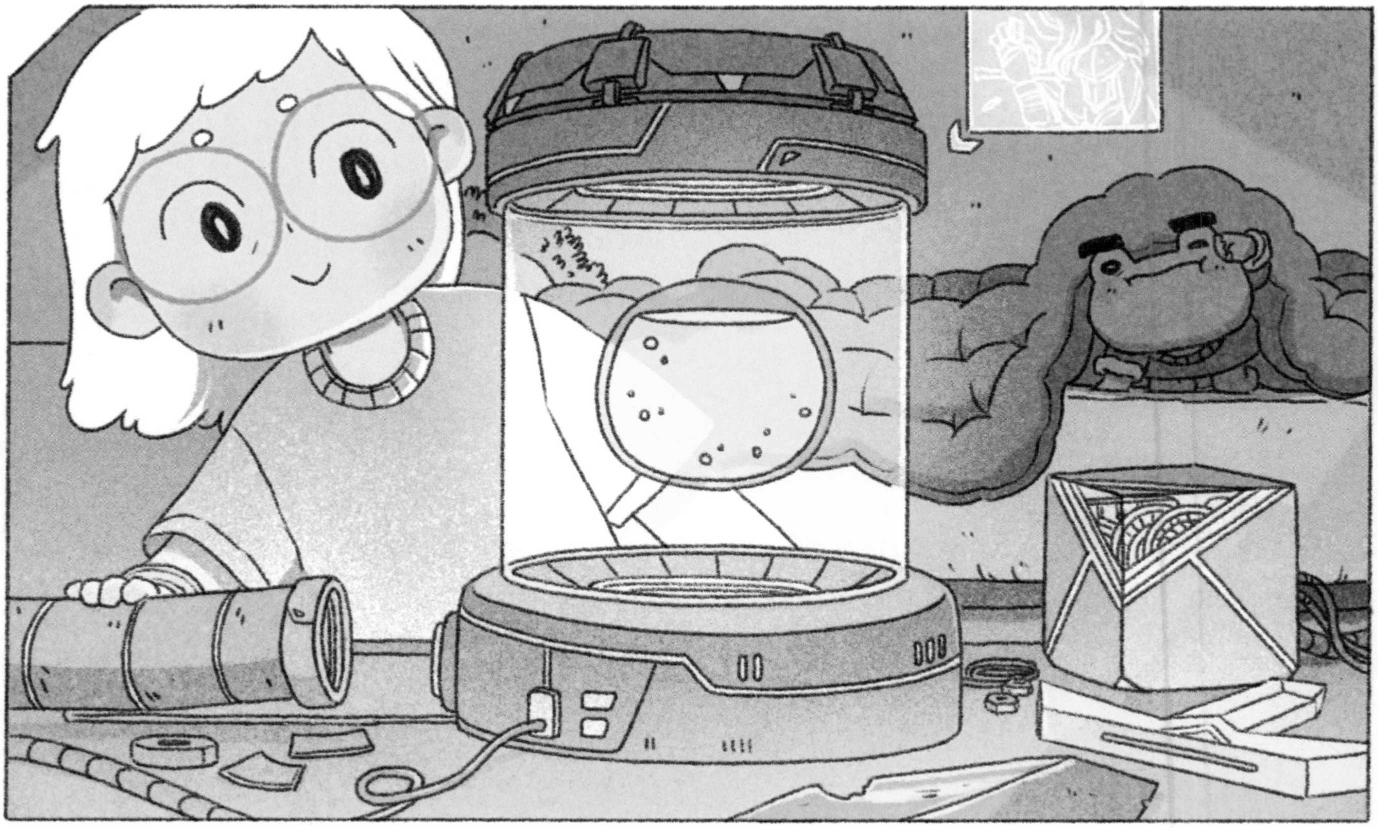

Could the Guardian Knights return? Their bravery amazed Juniper, she was astounded that they protected both the cityfolk and the tama-tamas from such deadly beasts.

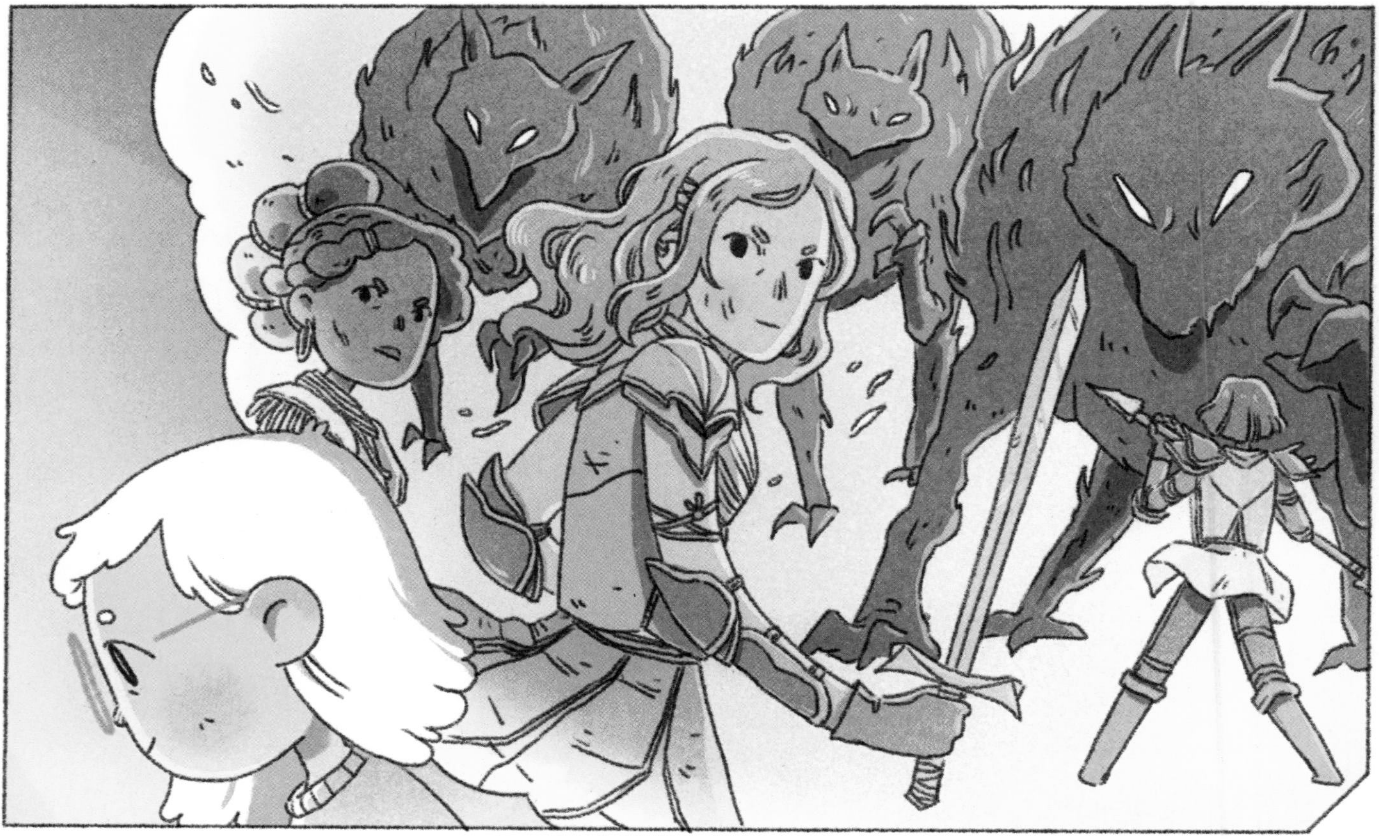

Soon, she started to imagine how it would feel to be one herself;
to protect the city and bring everyone together once more...

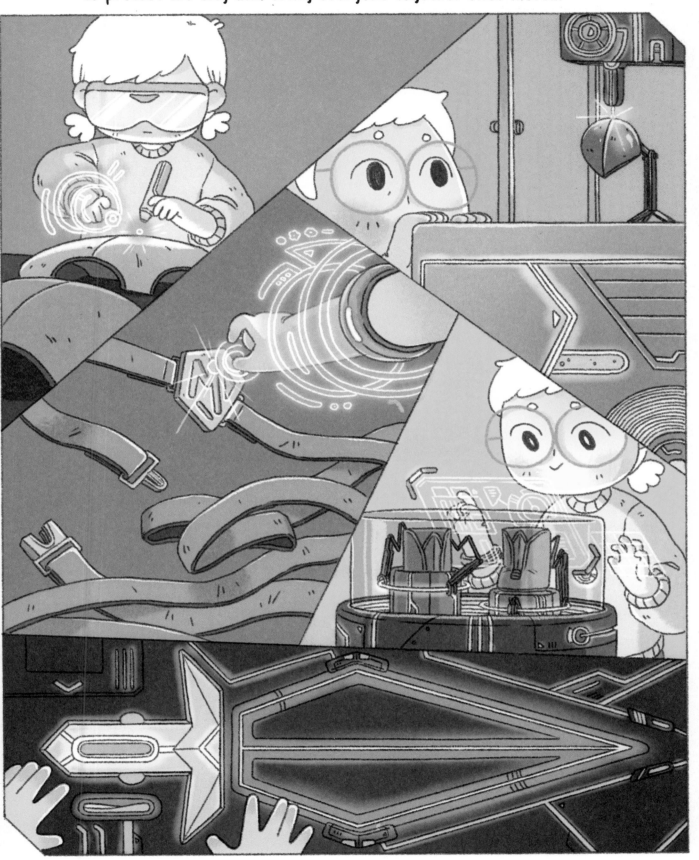

And after a morning of hard work, she had it:

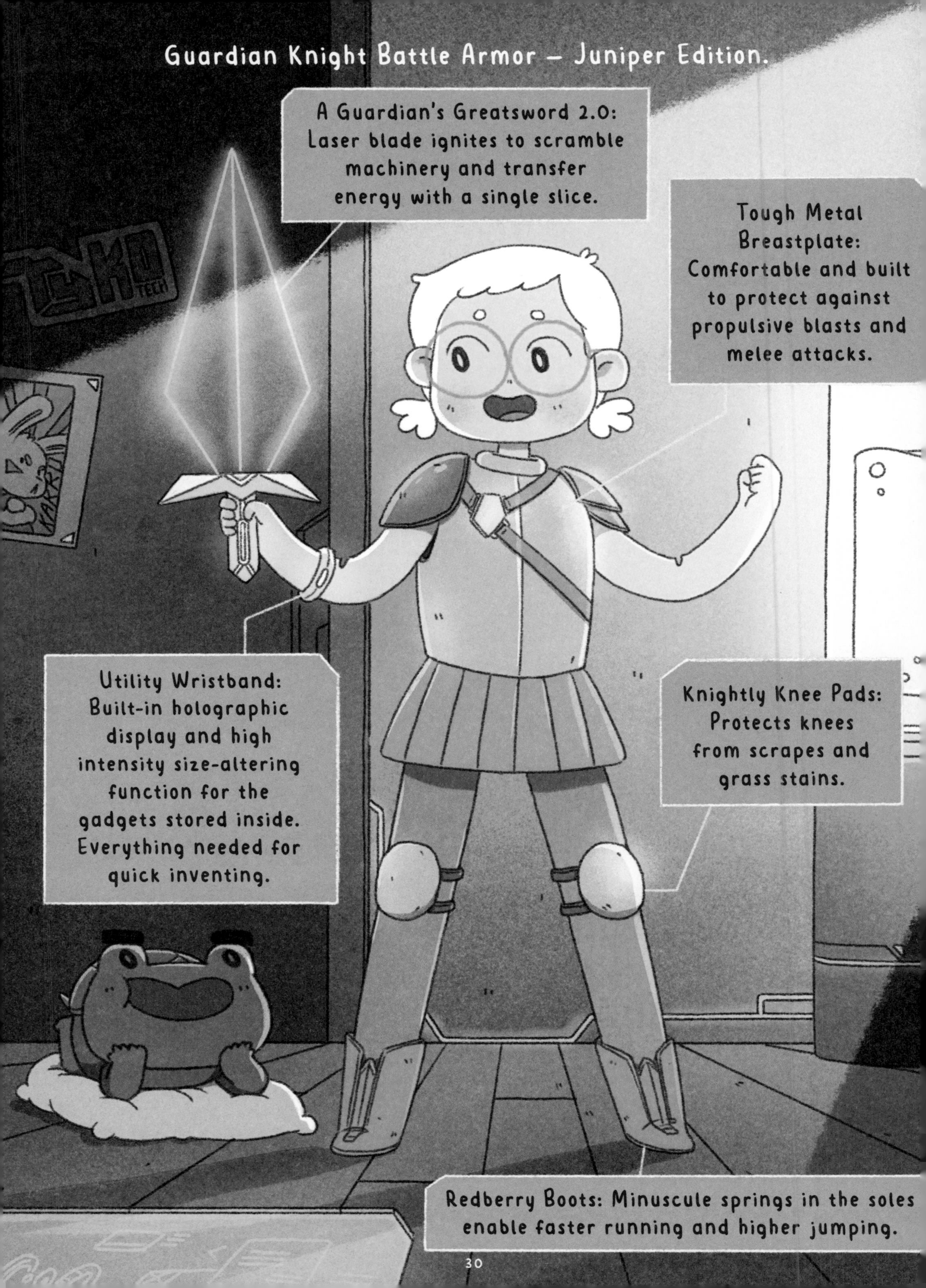
Guardian Knight Battle Armor – Juniper Edition.
A Guardian's Greatsword 2.0: Laser blade ignites to scramble machinery and transfer energy with a single slice.
Tough Metal Breastplate: Comfortable and built to protect against propulsive blasts and melee attacks.
Utility Wristband: Built-in holographic display and high intensity size-altering function for the gadgets stored inside. Everything needed for quick inventing.
Knightly Knee Pads: Protects knees from scrapes and grass stains.
Redberry Boots: Minuscule springs in the soles enable faster running and higher jumping.

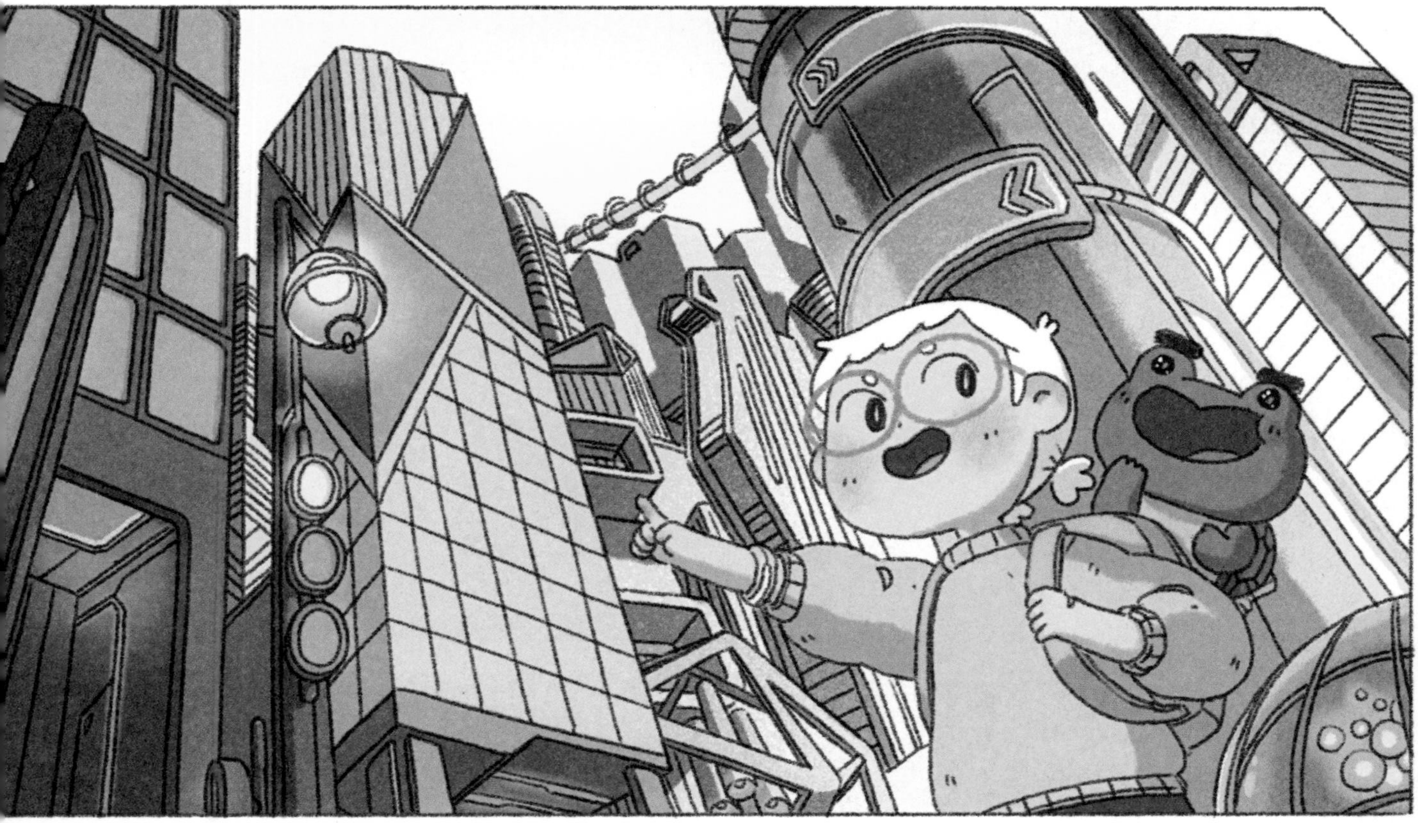

That afternoon, Juniper showed Albie all around the city, telling him what every sign meant, what every building was for, and where every cyber train came from.

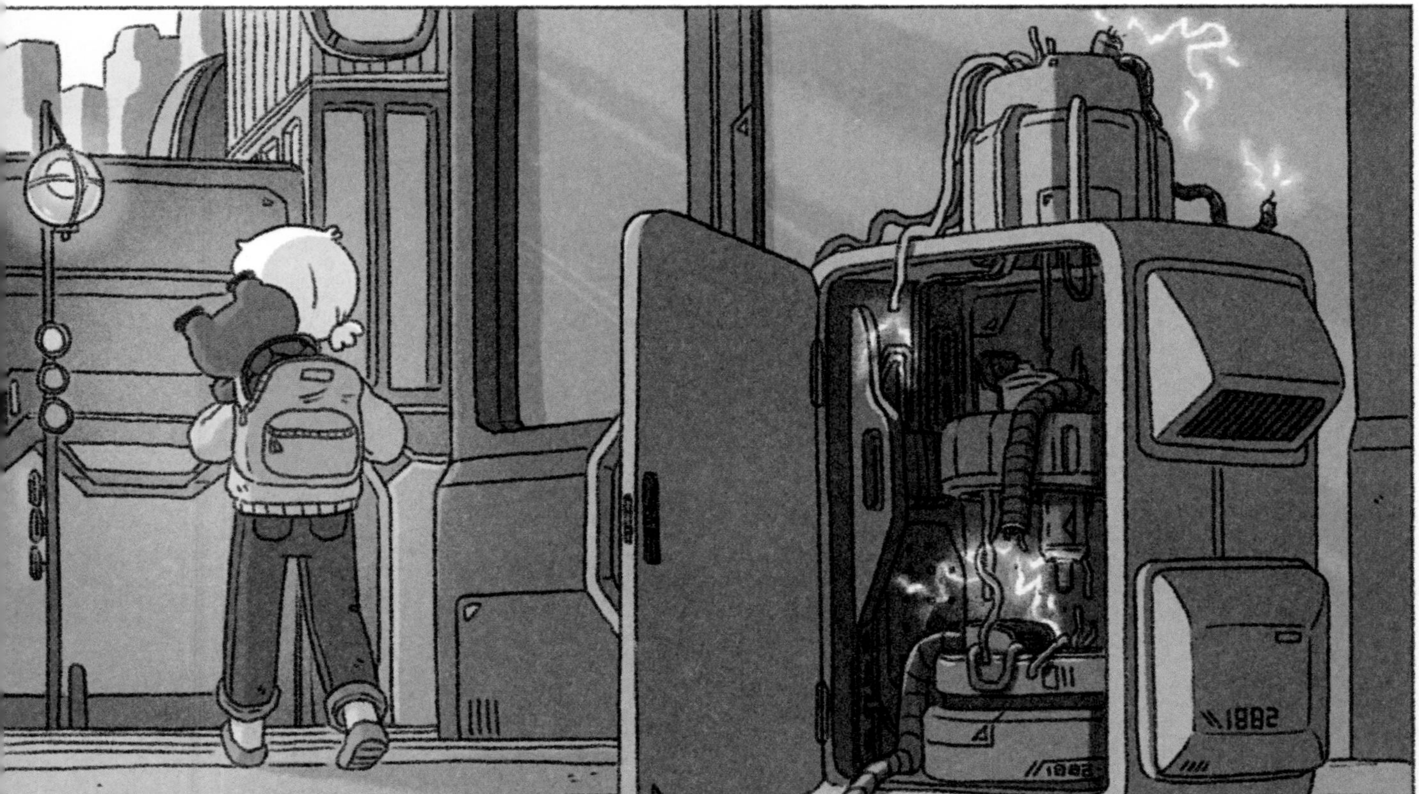

For the rest of the day, Juniper and Albie hung out while the young inventor figured out how the kabbage seeds worked. It took her several hours, but eventually...

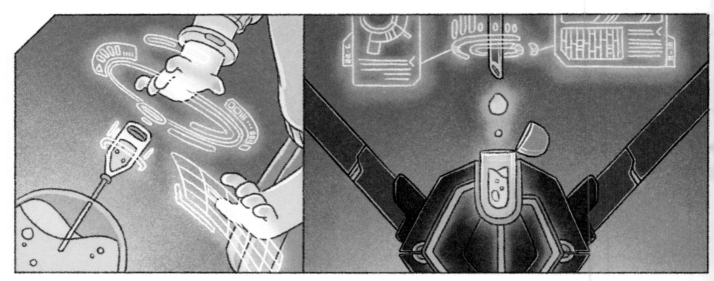

She had created a kabbage seed energy source! Just one drop could wirelessly power all of her inventions. Perhaps she could show it to President Kozen at Tykotech Corp, and she'd be the youngest inventor—

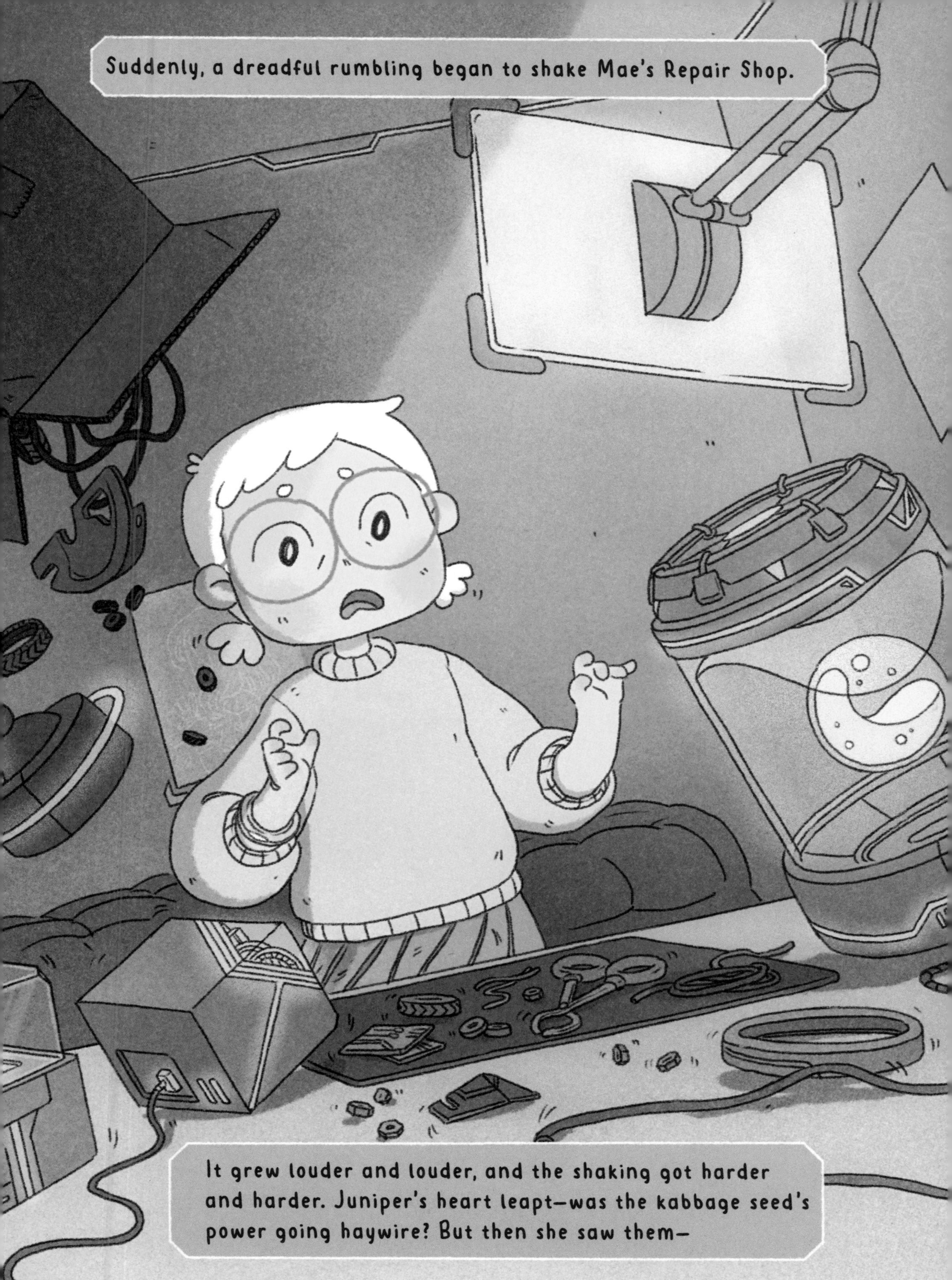
Suddenly, a dreadful rumbling began to shake Mae's Repair Shop.
It grew louder and louder, and the shaking got harder and harder. Juniper's heart leapt—was the kabbage seed's power going haywire? But then she saw them—

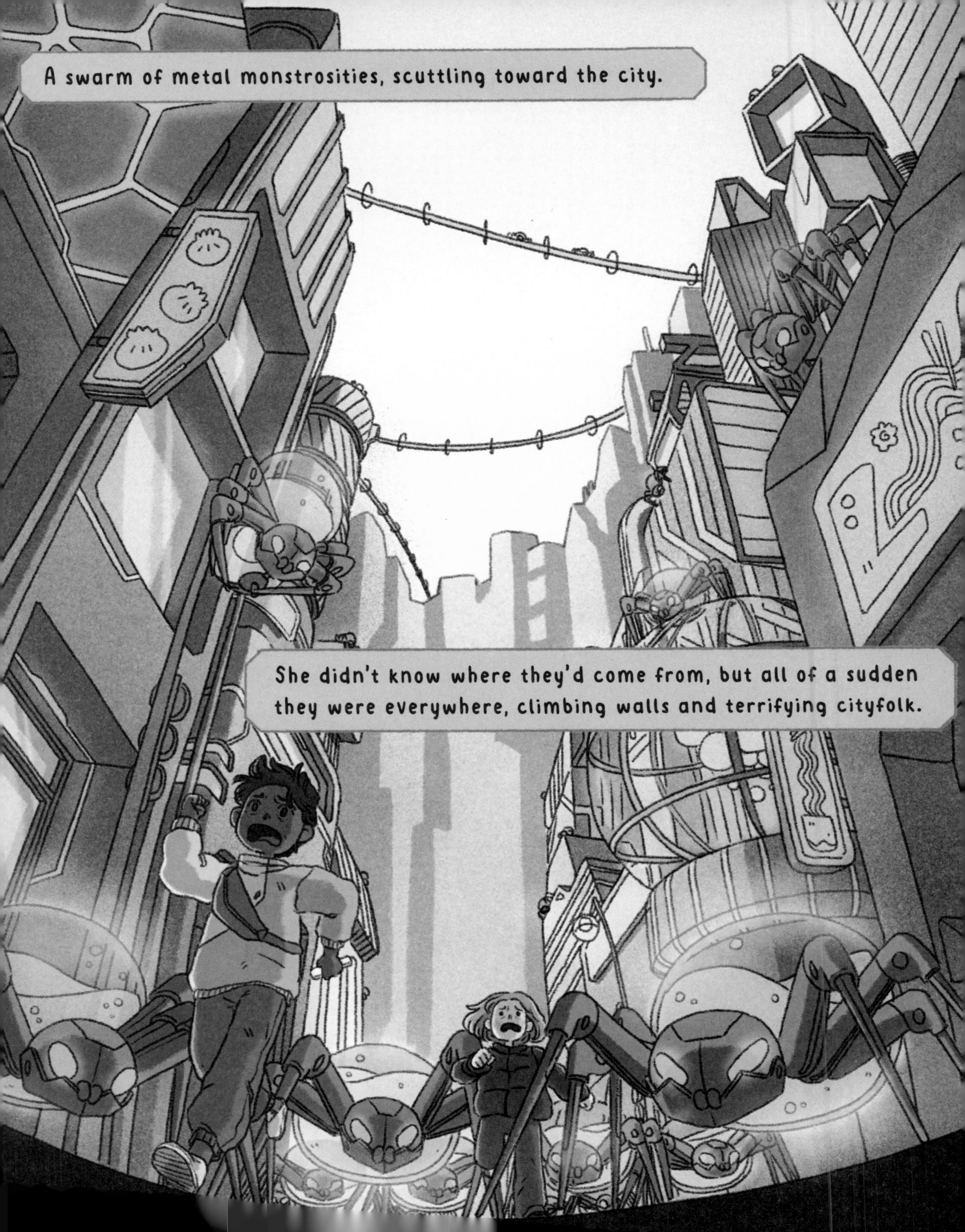
A swarm of metal monstrosities, scuttling toward the city.
She didn't know where they'd come from, but all of a sudden they were everywhere, climbing walls and terrifying cityfolk.

Juniper watched from her window in horror as they advanced on The Core. The insectoids dug their jaws into the city's power source...

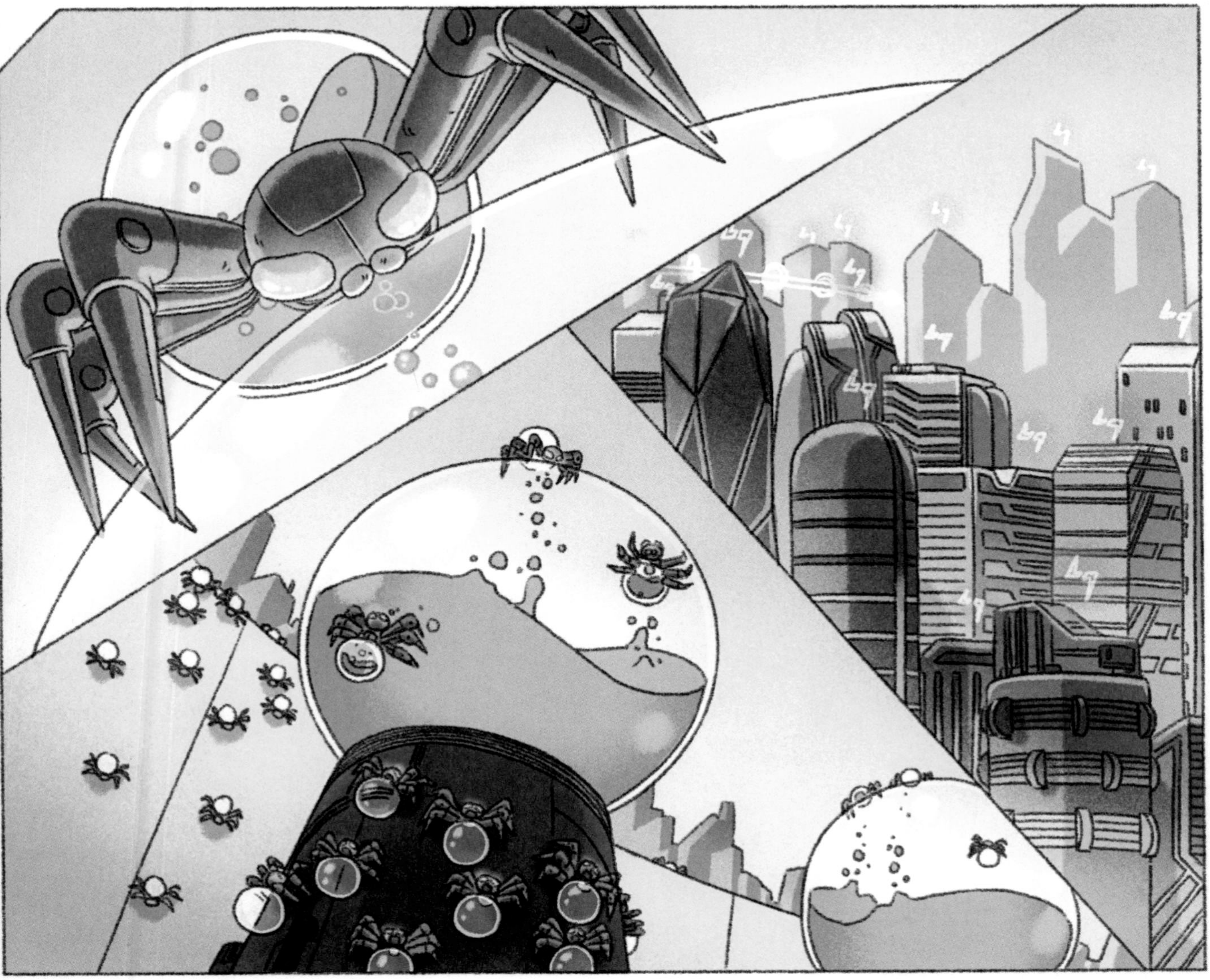

... And sucked all of the power from The Core! These evil bugs must have been draining the city of energy this whole time, and causing the awful power cuts. There was only one thing for Juniper to do.

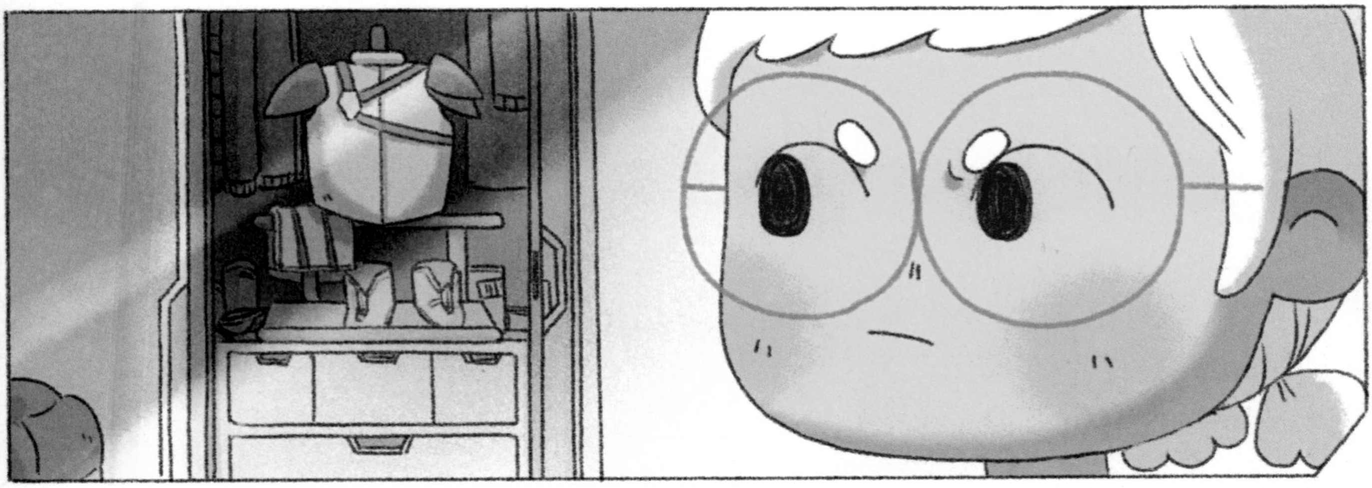

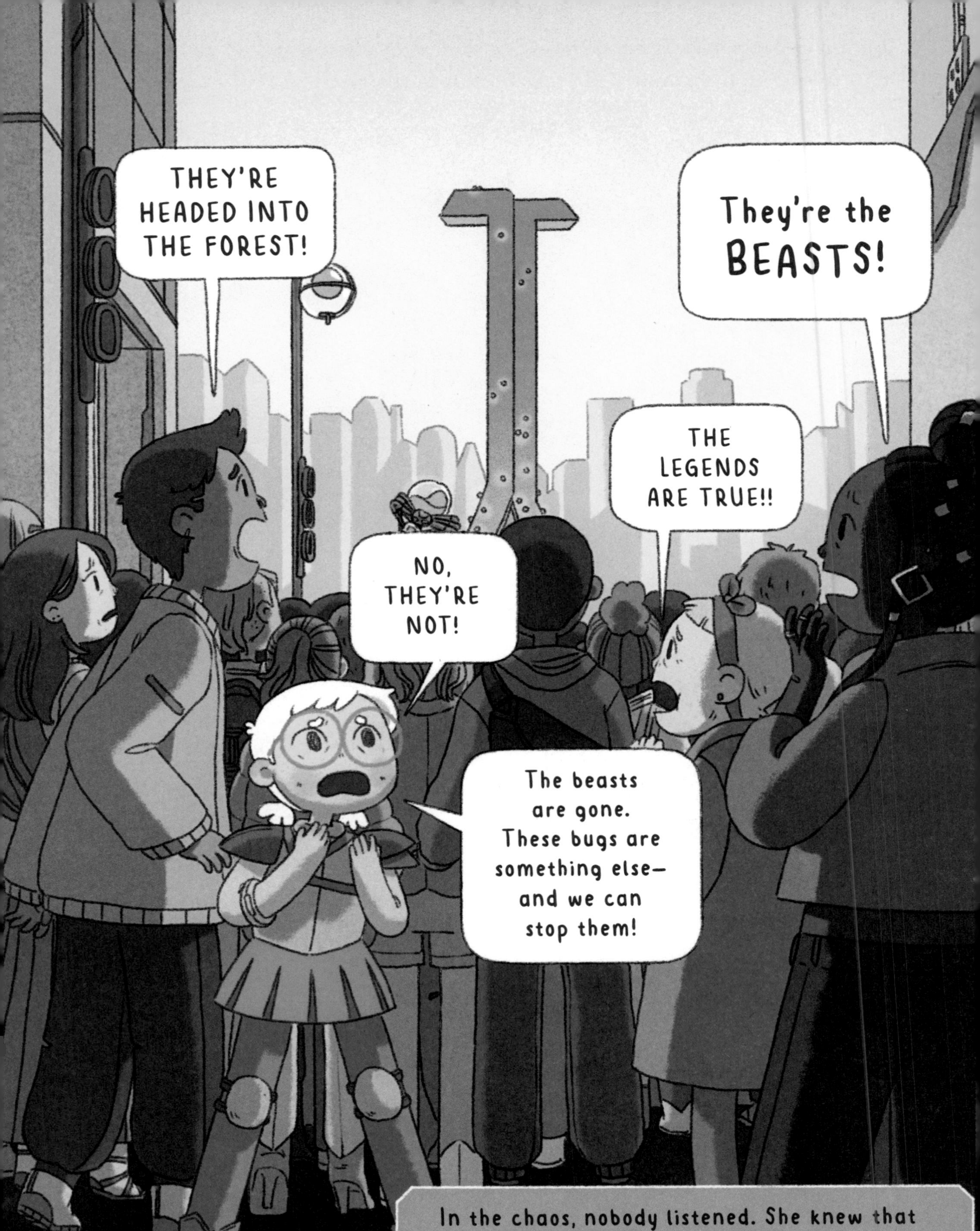
THEY'RE HEADED INTO THE FOREST!
They're the BEASTS!
THE LEGENDS ARE TRUE!!
NO, THEY'RE NOT!
The beasts are gone. These bugs are something else—and we can stop them!
In the chaos, nobody listened. She knew that she would have to face the insectoids herself.

Lucky for Juniper Mae, one of the insectoids had left something behind, and Albie was there to help.

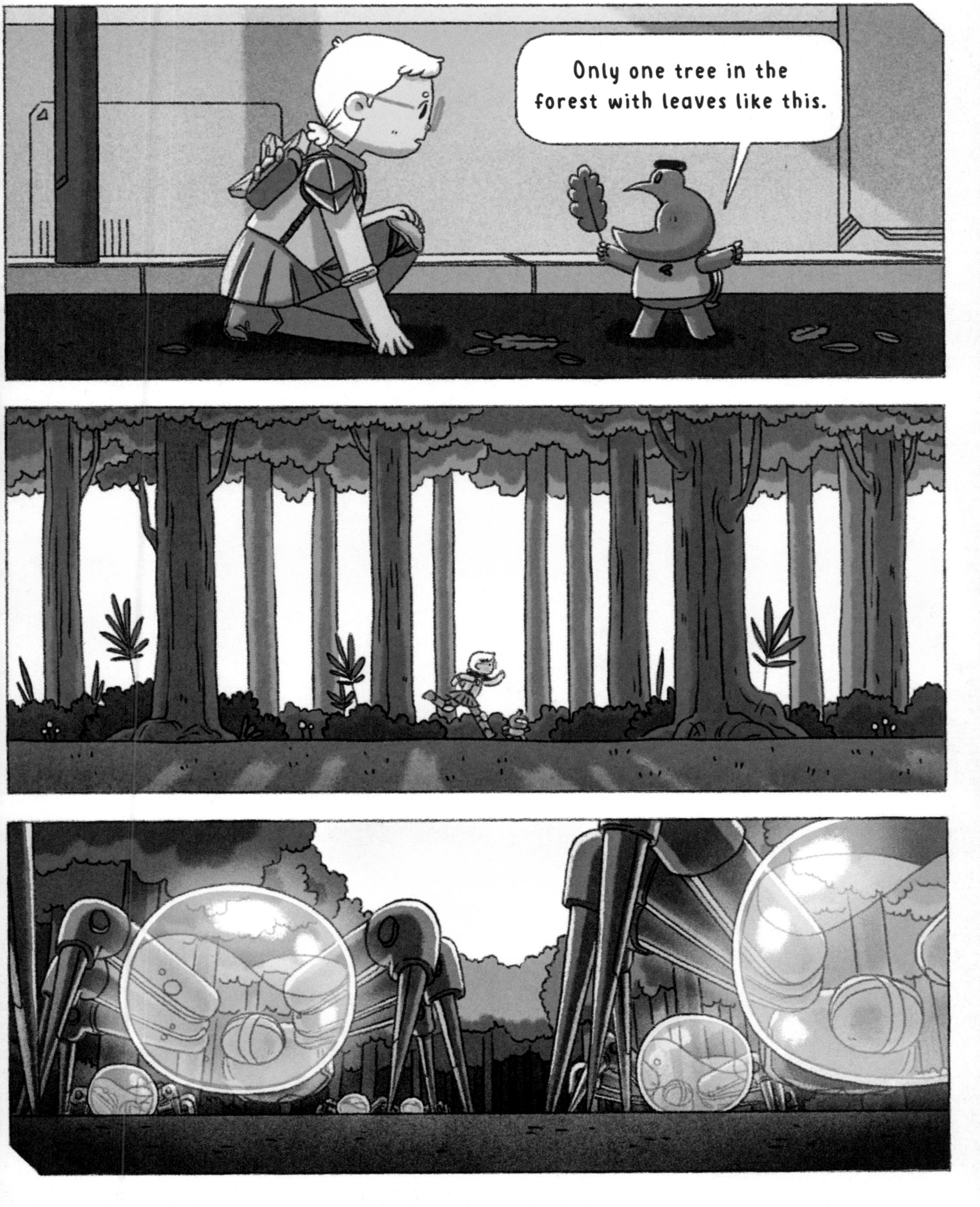
Only one tree in the forest with leaves like this.

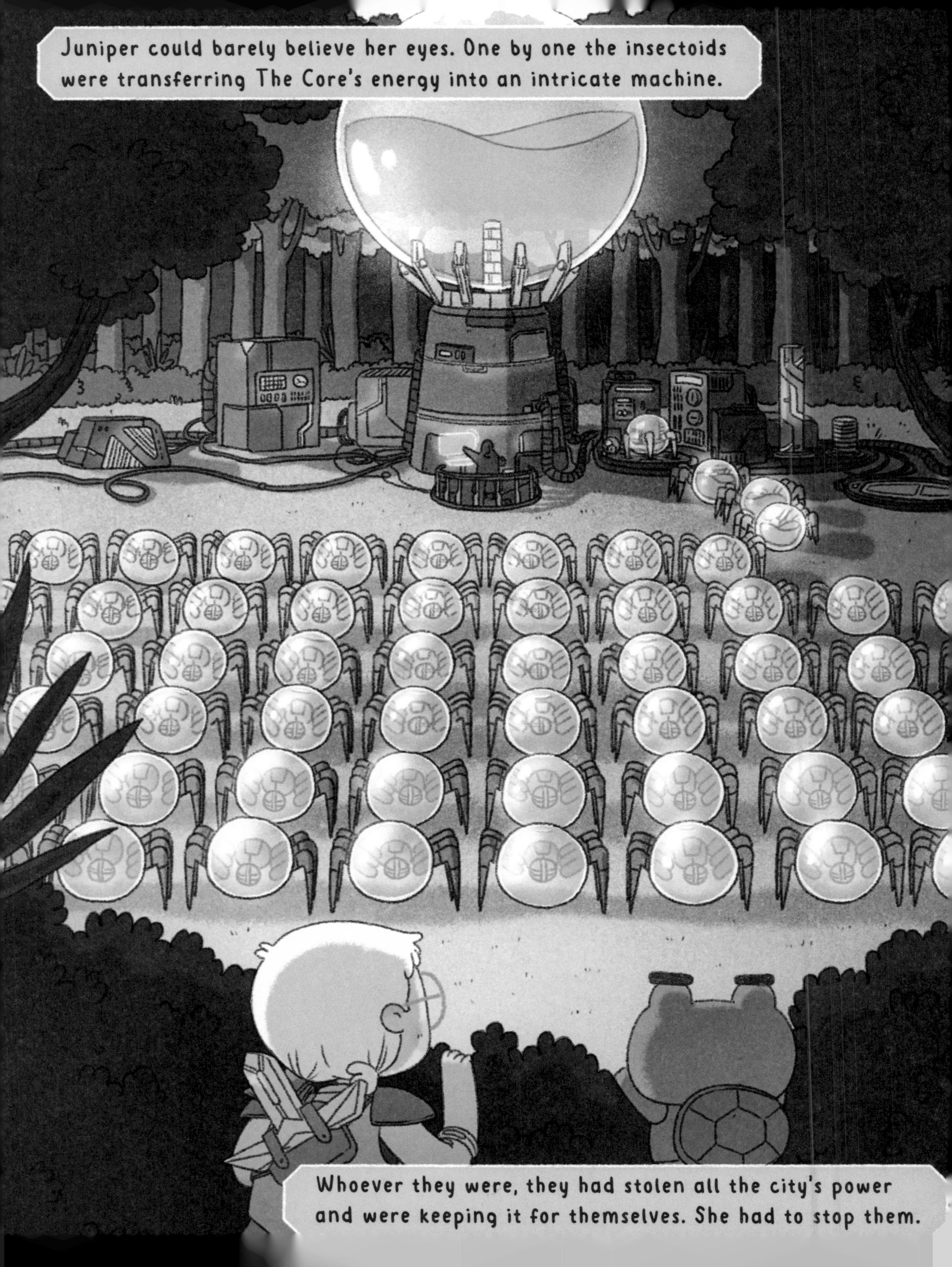
Juniper could barely believe her eyes. One by one the insectoids were transferring The Core's energy into an intricate machine.
Whoever they were, they had stolen all the city's power and were keeping it for themselves. She had to stop them.

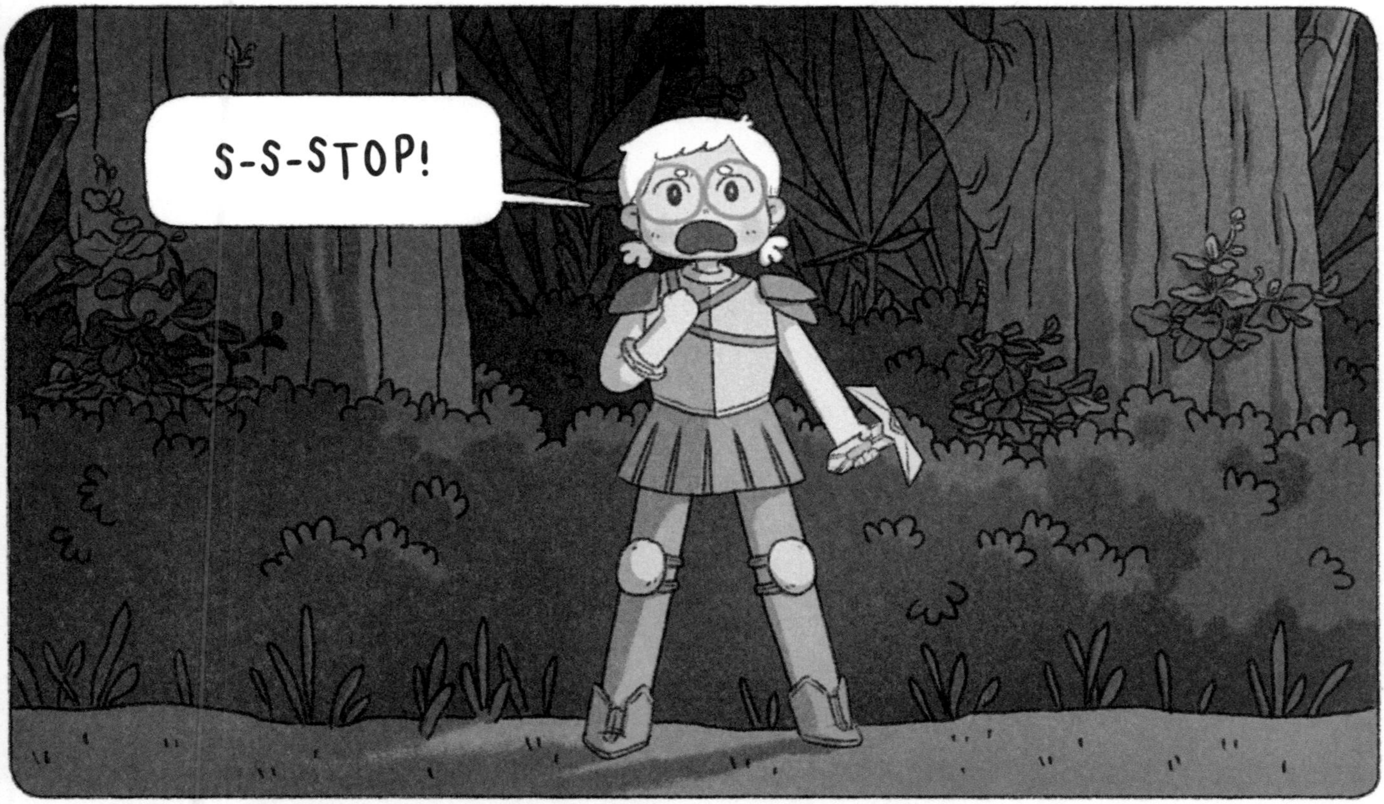
S-S-STOP!

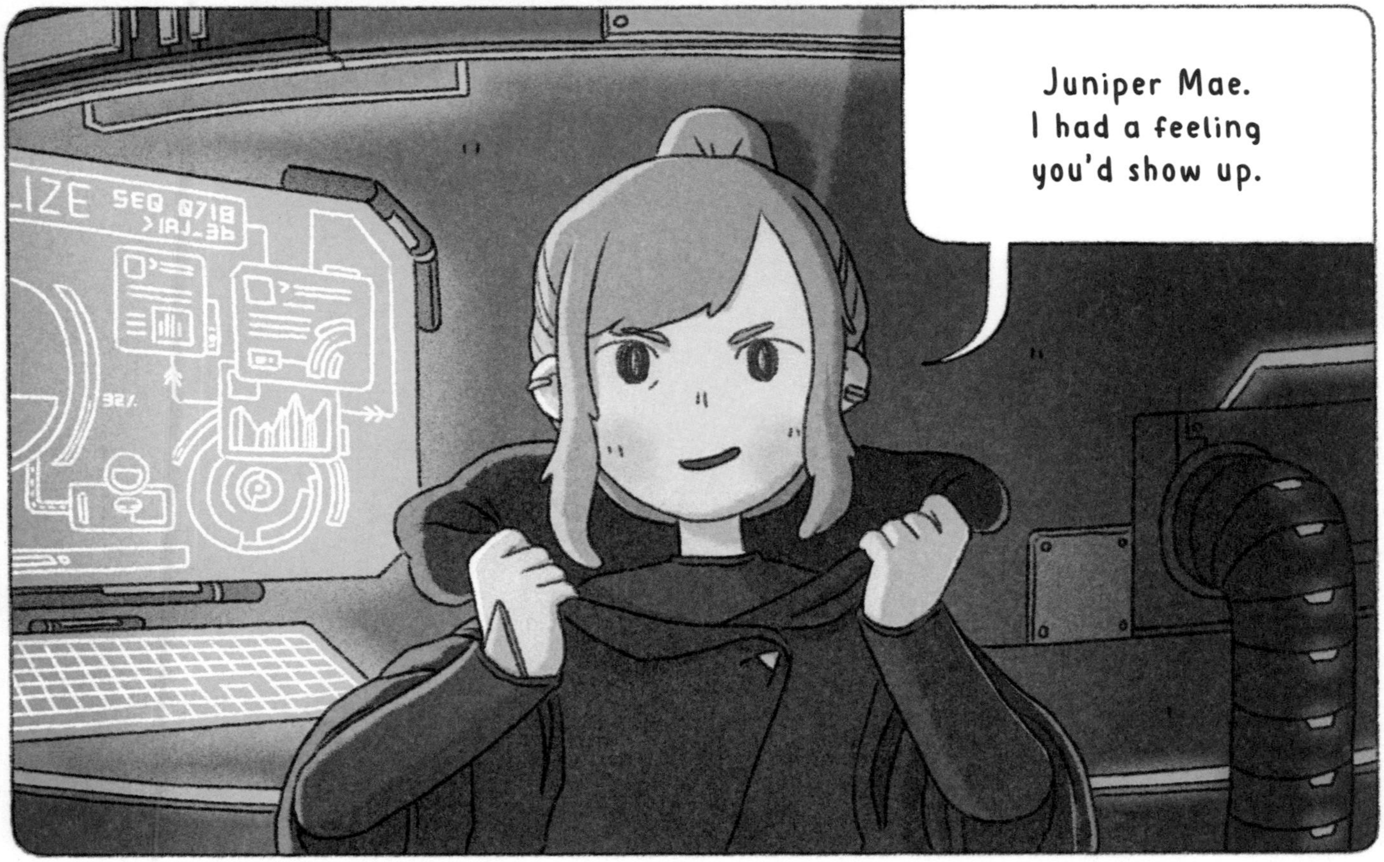
Juniper Mae.
I had a feeling
you'd show up.
LIZE SEQ 0718
>IAJ_3b

To Juniper's surprise, she recognized the daughter of President Kozen, Kaya Kozen. Why would the President of Tykotech Corp's daughter steal the energy from The Core? From everyone in the city? It made no sense!

"I've been watching you ever since you crash-landed here."
Kaya said, "We're similar, you and I..."

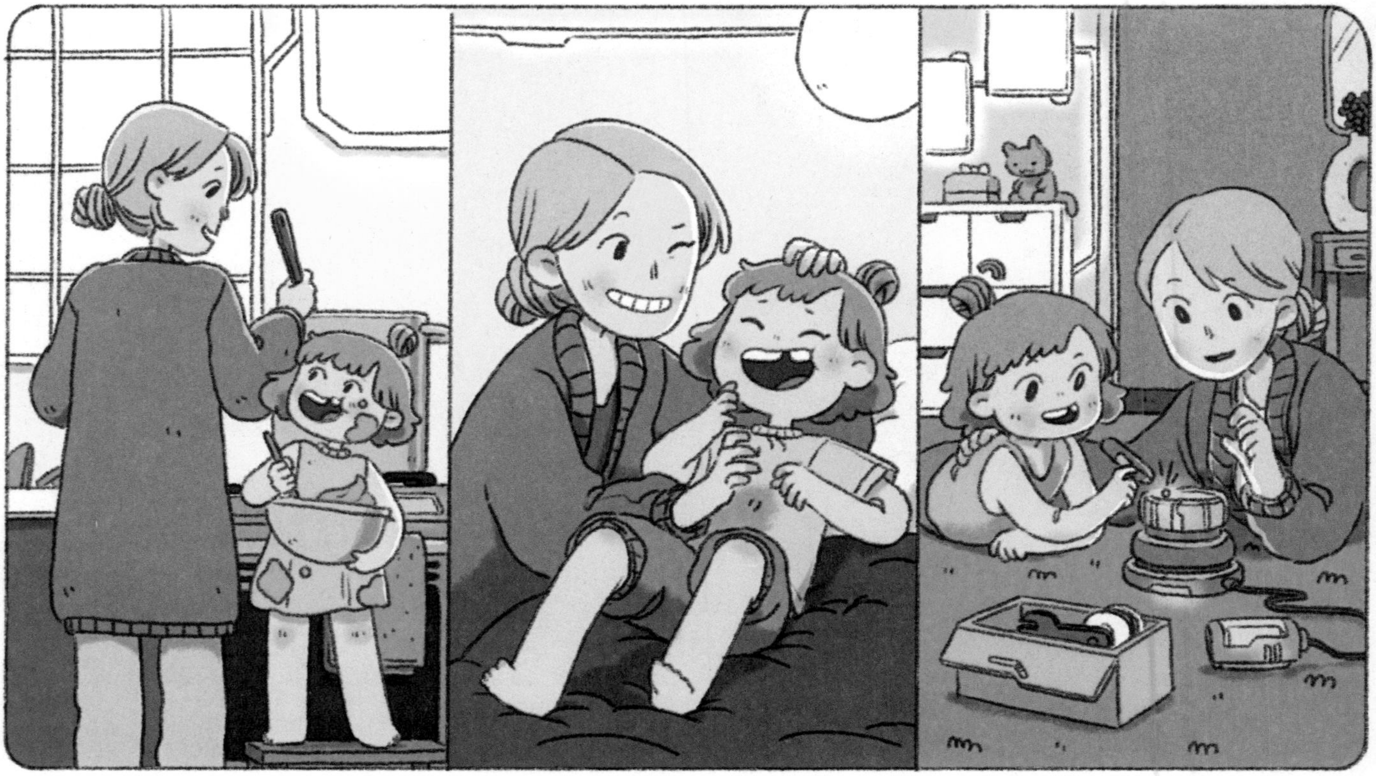

"You see, my mom and I used to do everything together.
But then The Core's power cuts started."

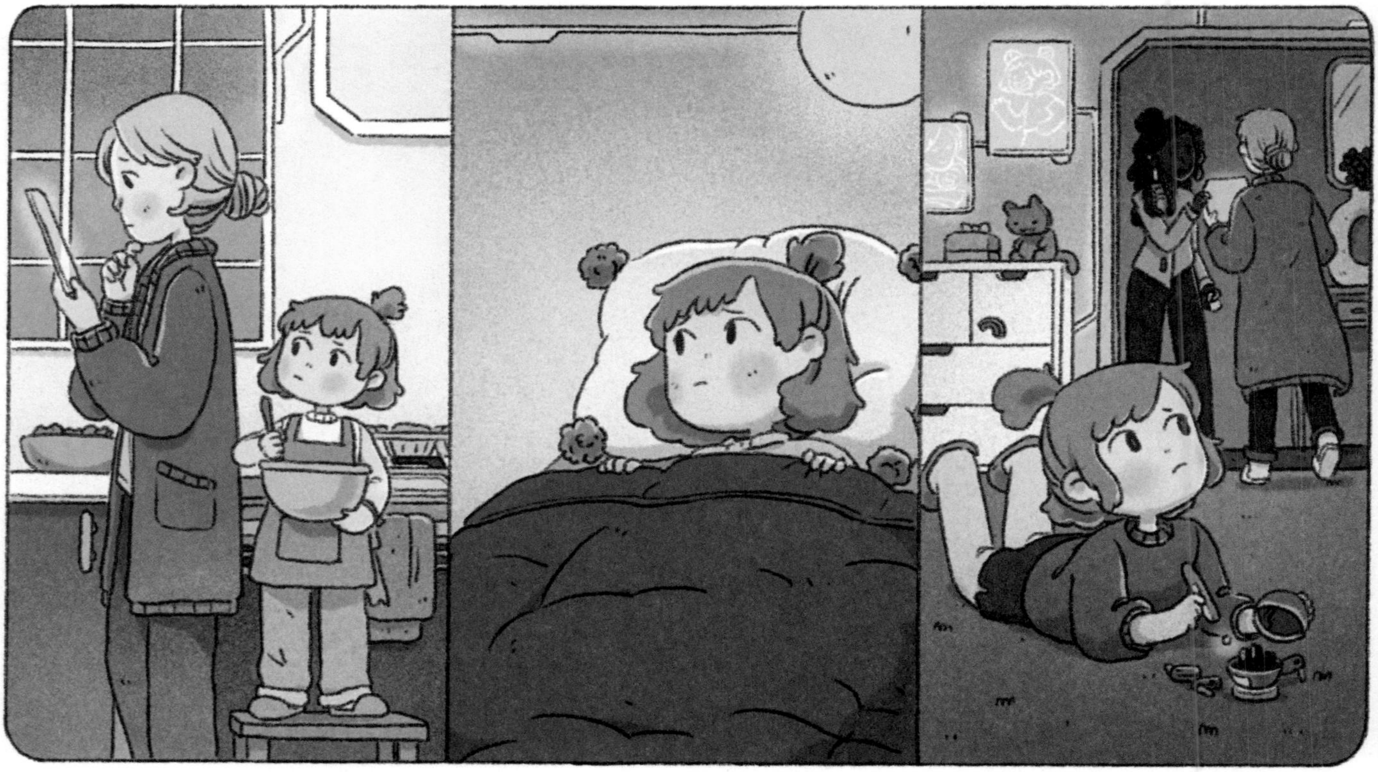

"The stupid outages kept happening, and she got so busy trying to fix them, that she forgot to spend any time with me."

"I felt so lonely and unwanted, I started spending all day in my room, inventing things. Just like you do."

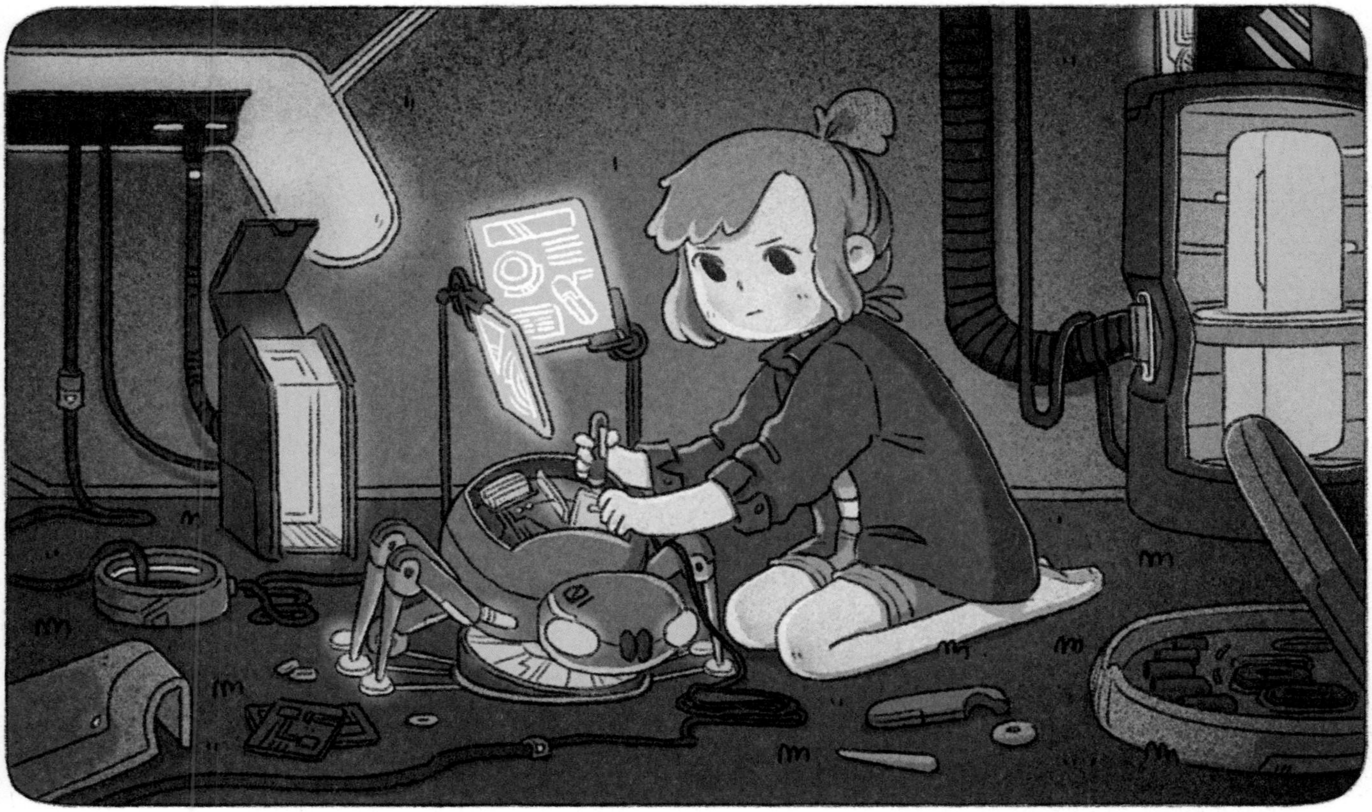

"And now I have all the city's power, I'll give it right back to them, claiming I've invented a new power source."

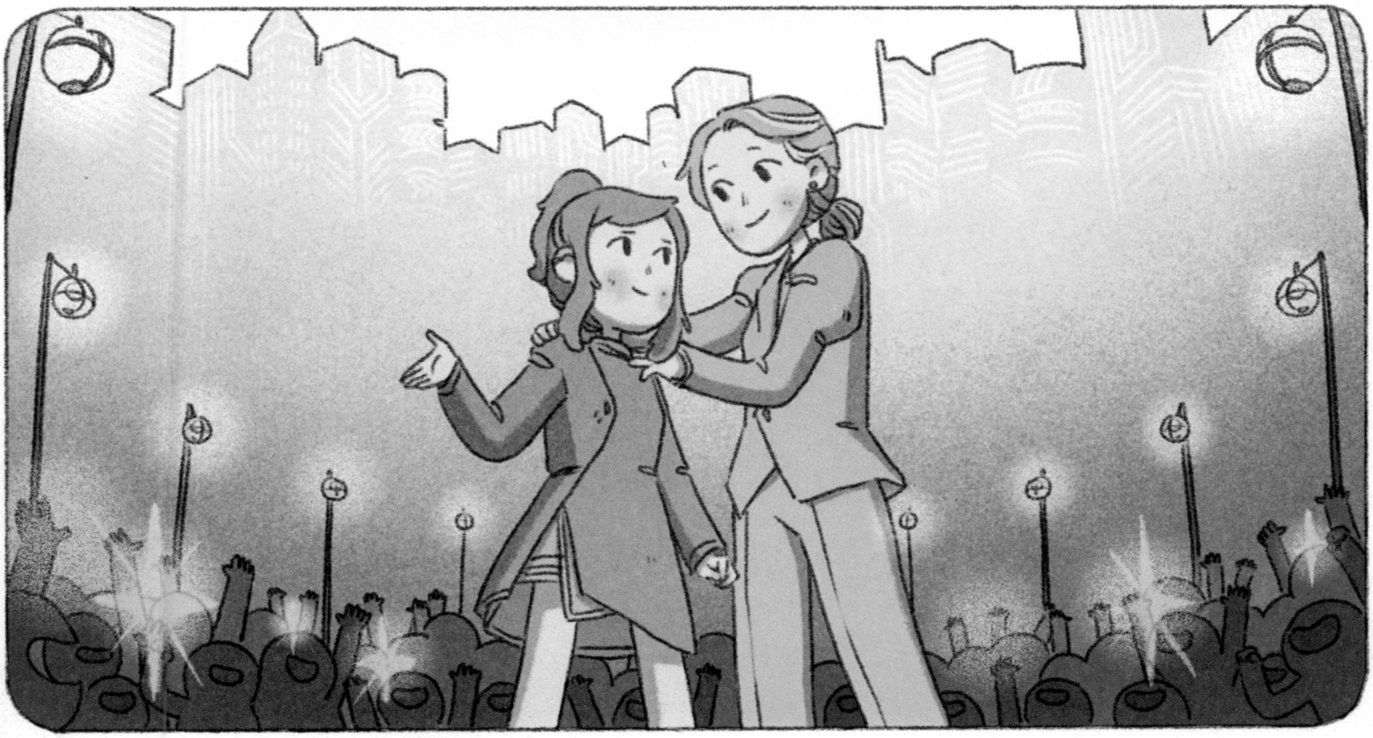

"I'll be a hero. My mom will be proud, and I'll never be lonely again."

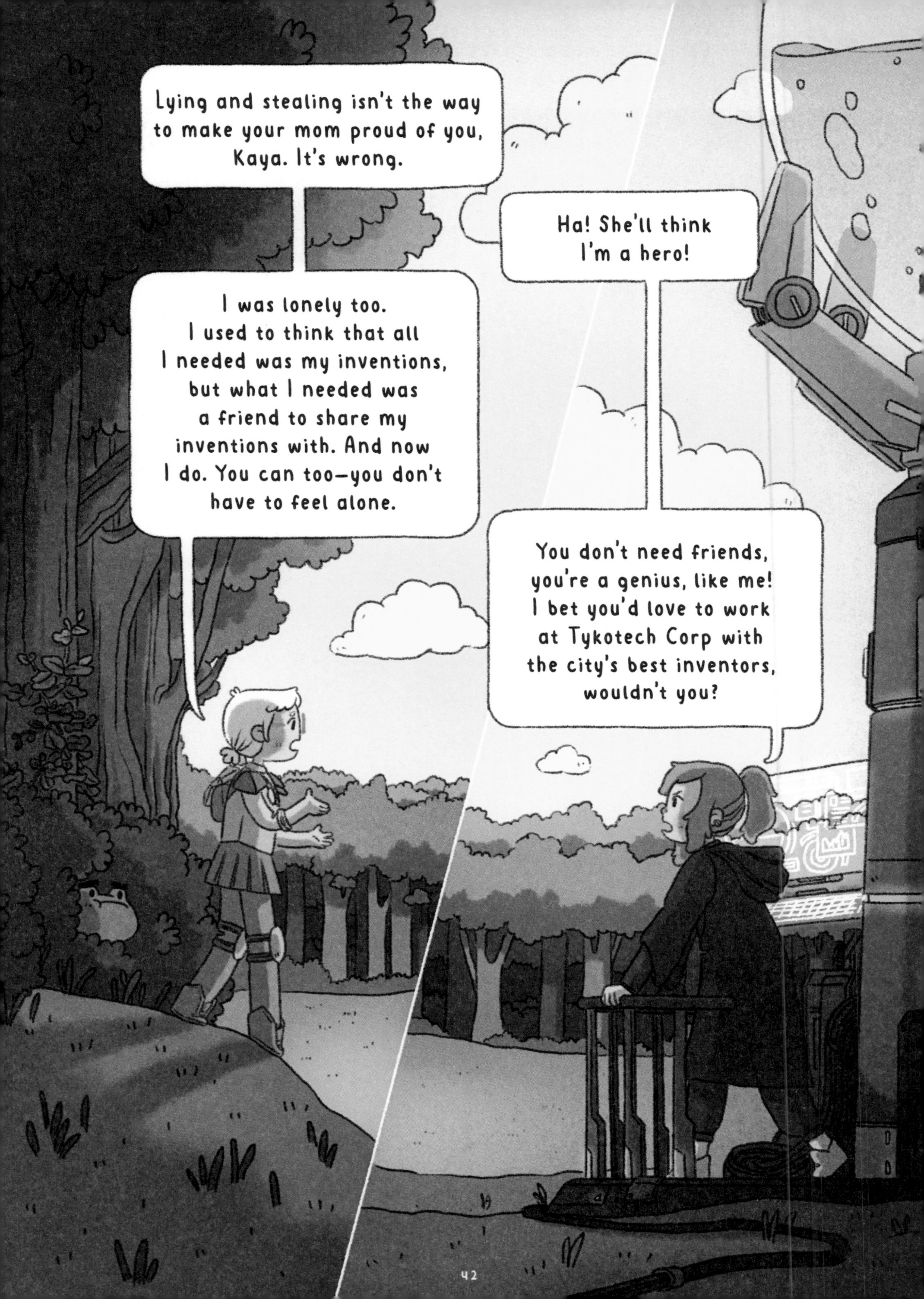
Lying and stealing isn't the way to make your mom proud of you, Kaya. It's wrong.
I was lonely too. I used to think that all I needed was my inventions, but what I needed was a friend to share my inventions with. And now I do. You can too—you don't have to feel alone.
Ha! She'll think I'm a hero!
You don't need friends, you're a genius, like me! I bet you'd love to work at Tykotech Corp with the city's best inventors, wouldn't you?

"I can make that happen in an instant," Kaya continued, "All you have to do is go back home and forget what you've seen here. What do you say?"

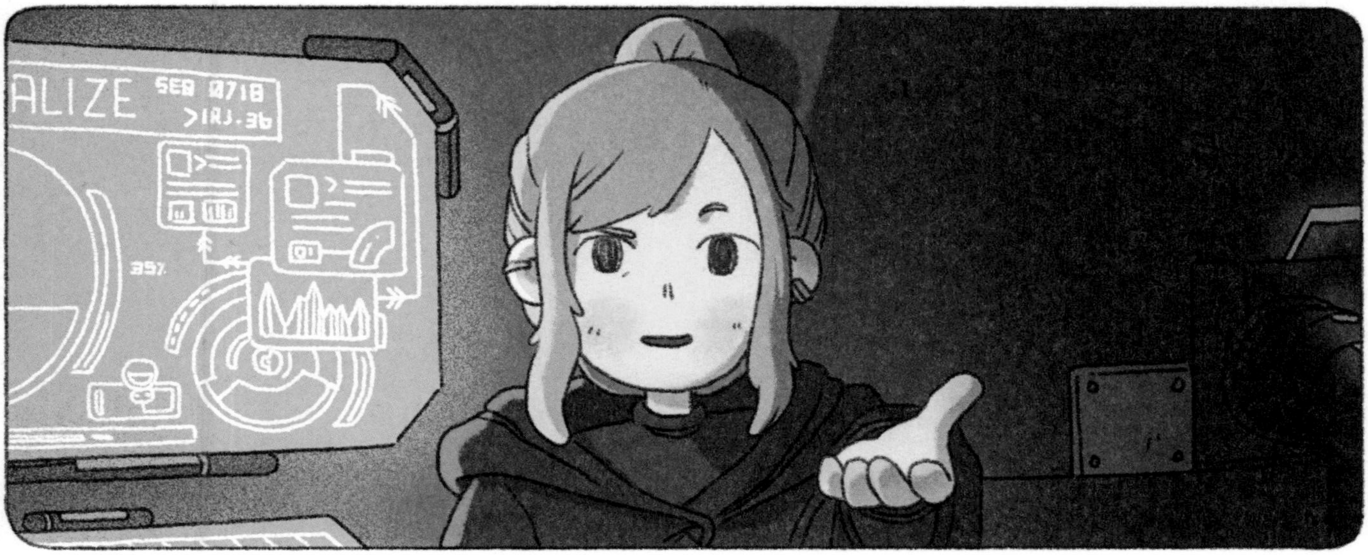
ALIZE

It was all Juniper had ever wanted. If Kaya hadn't been the cause of the power cuts, Juniper could find a way to solve them herself.

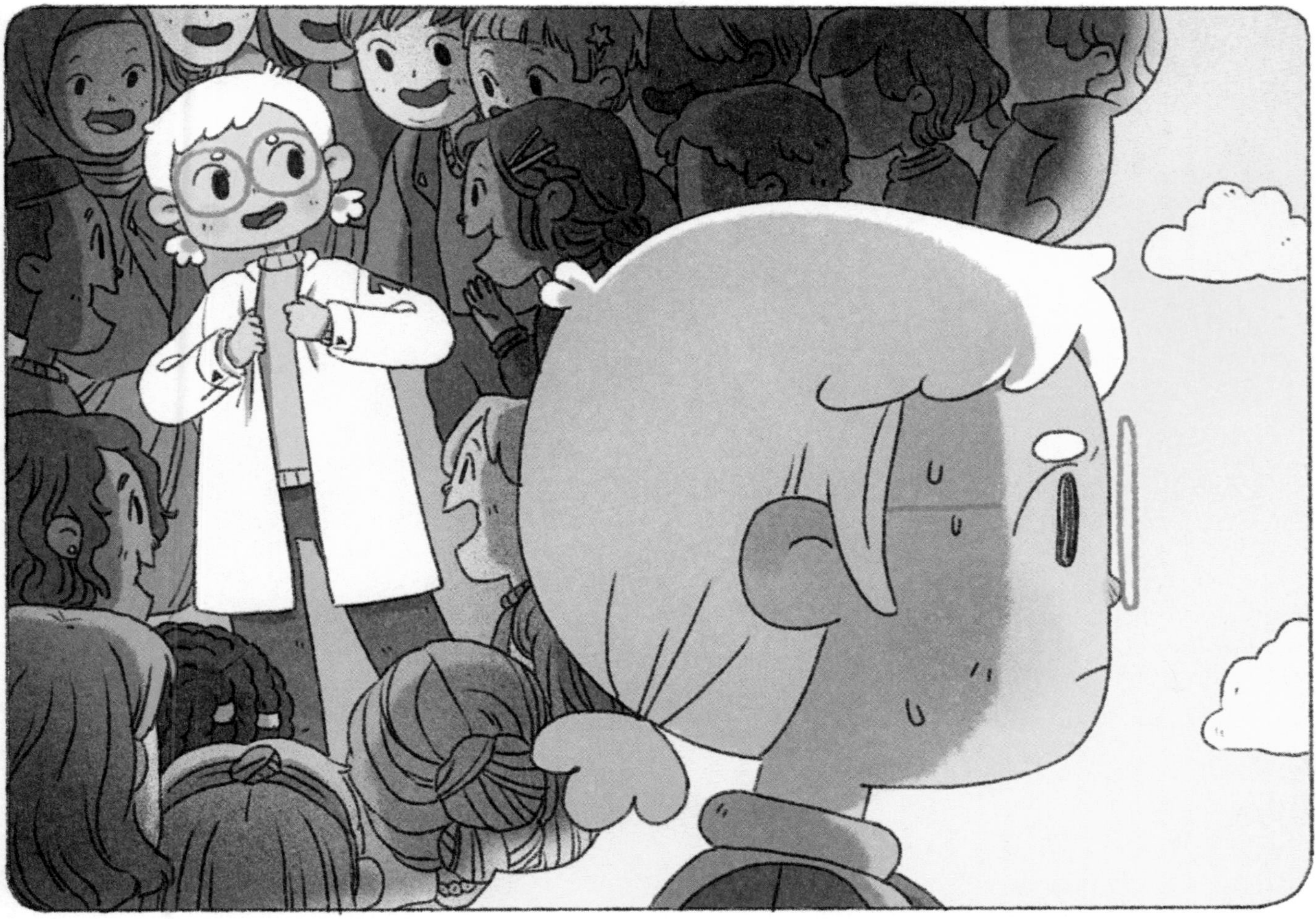

Kids from all over would want to be her friend then. But that would mean letting Kaya Kozen get away with her crimes. Could Juniper really allow that to happen?

Then she saw her new friend's fearful little face.

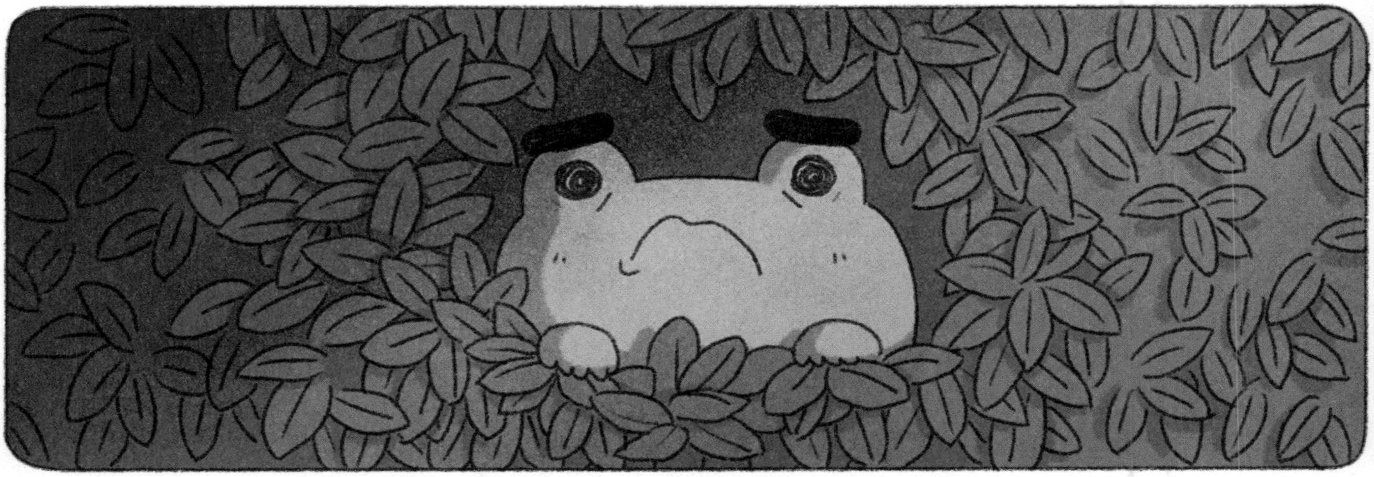

She remembered that the Guardian Knights defended the tama-tamas and cityfolk from all danger. And Kaya was dangerous.

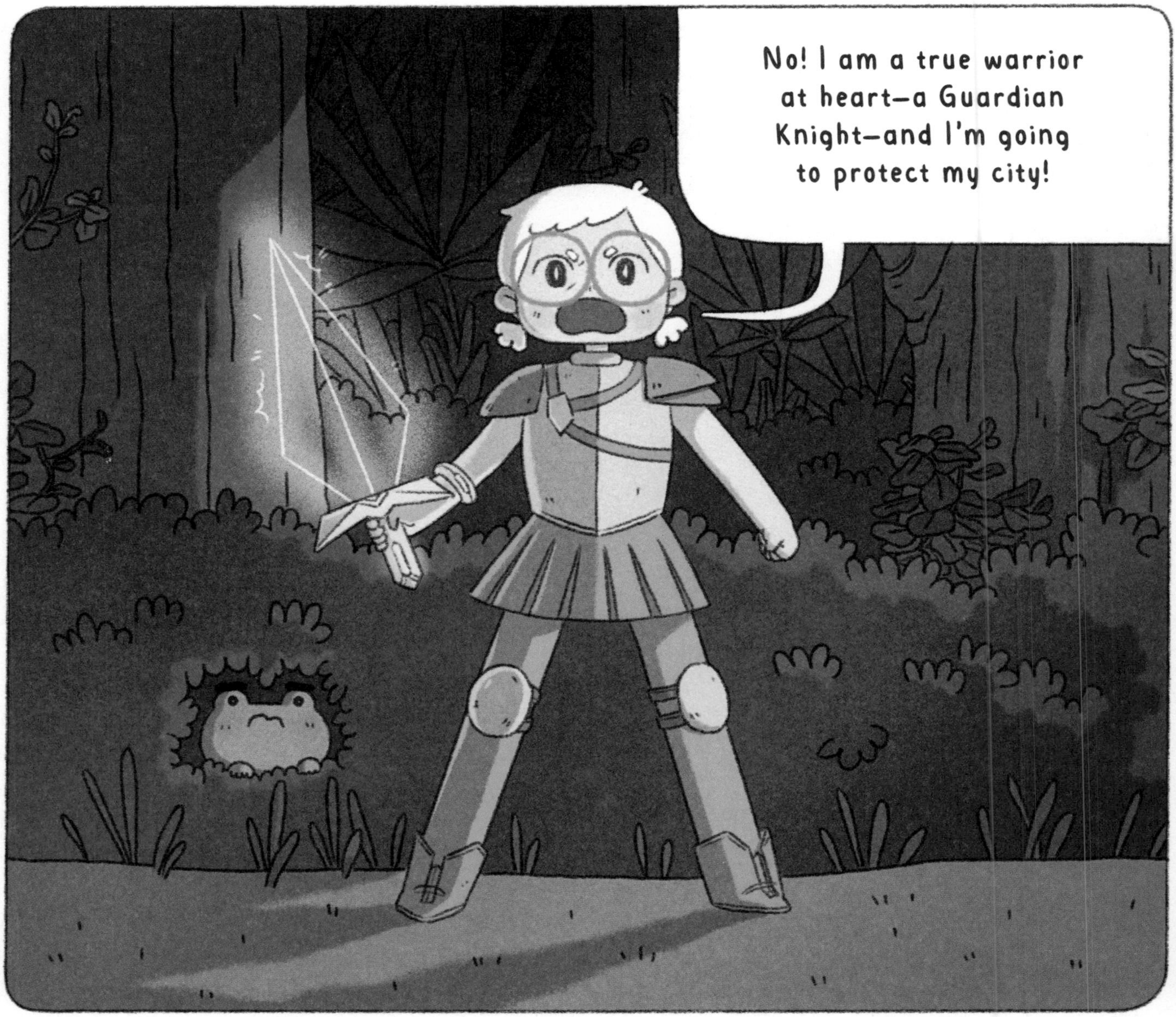
No! I am a true warrior at heart—a Guardian Knight—and I'm going to protect my city!

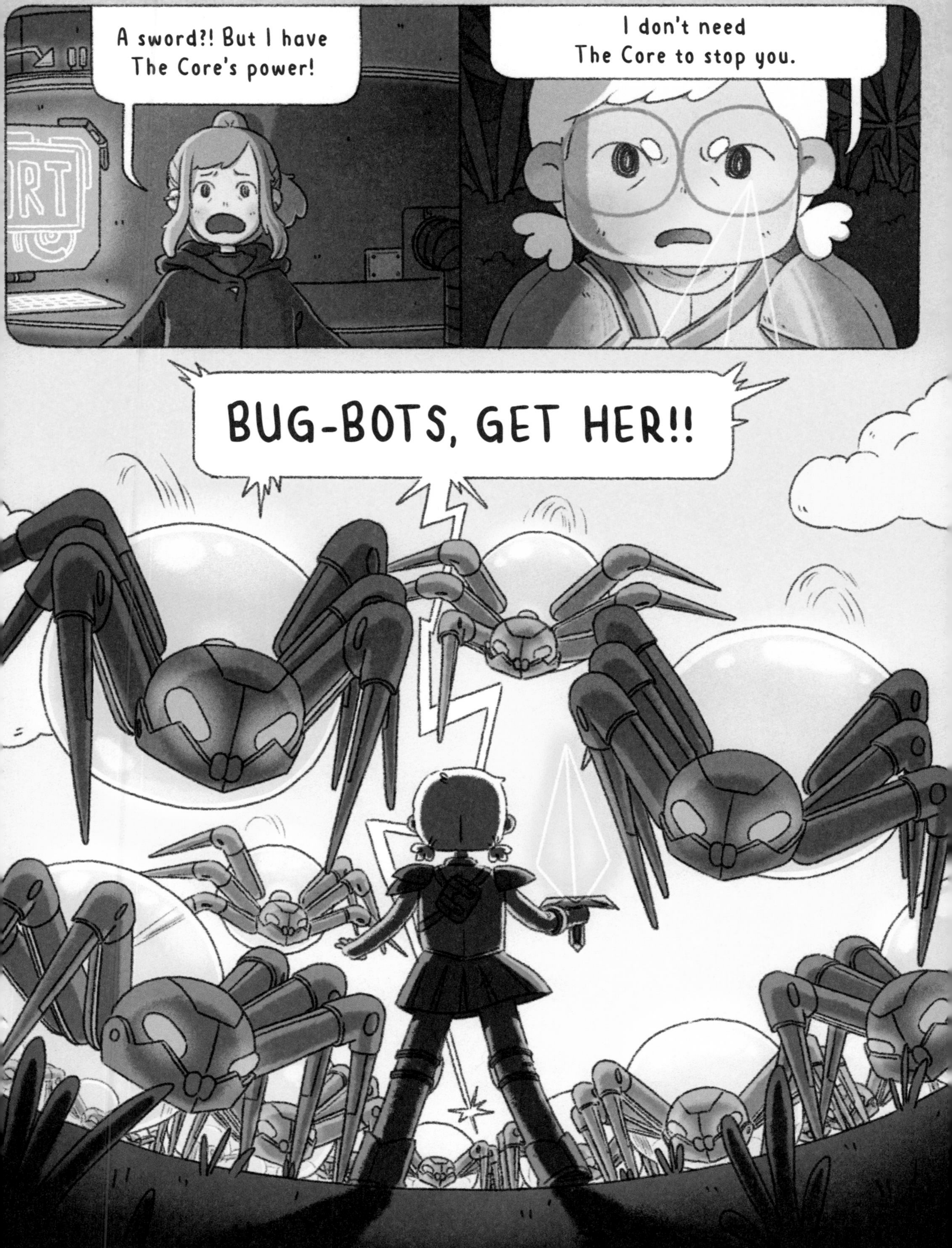
A sword?! But I have The Core's power!
I don't need The Core to stop you.
BUG-BOTS, GET HER!!

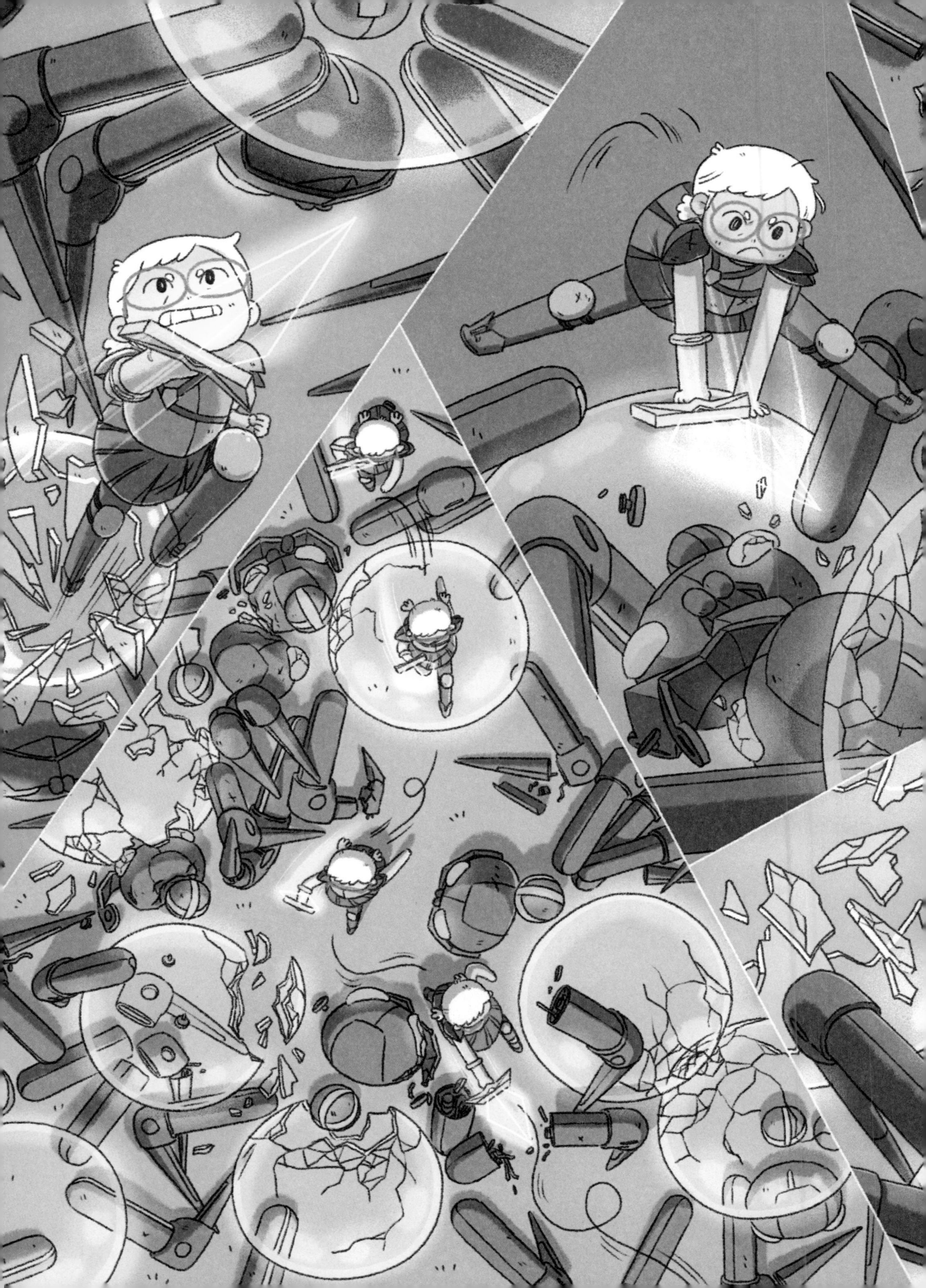

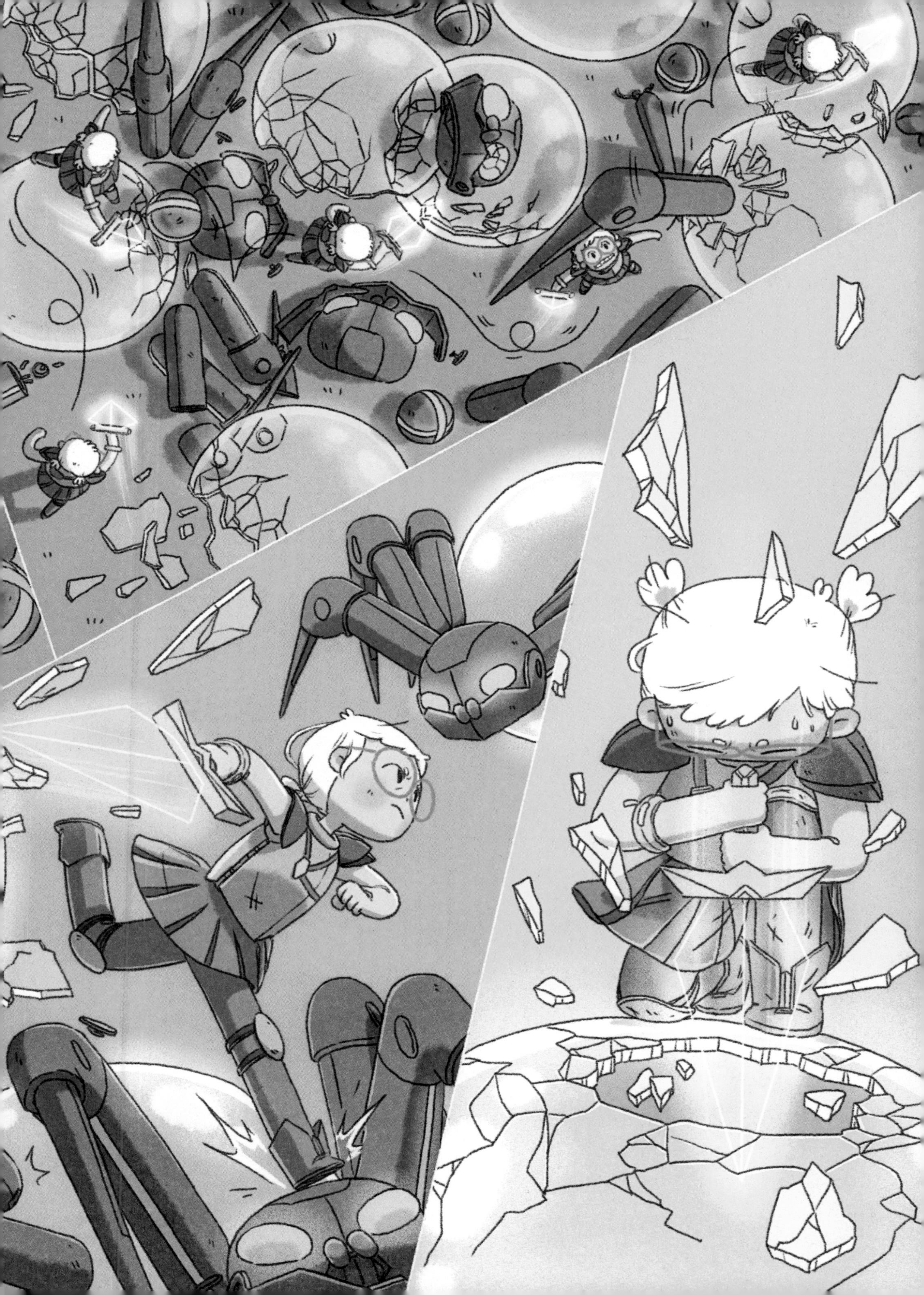

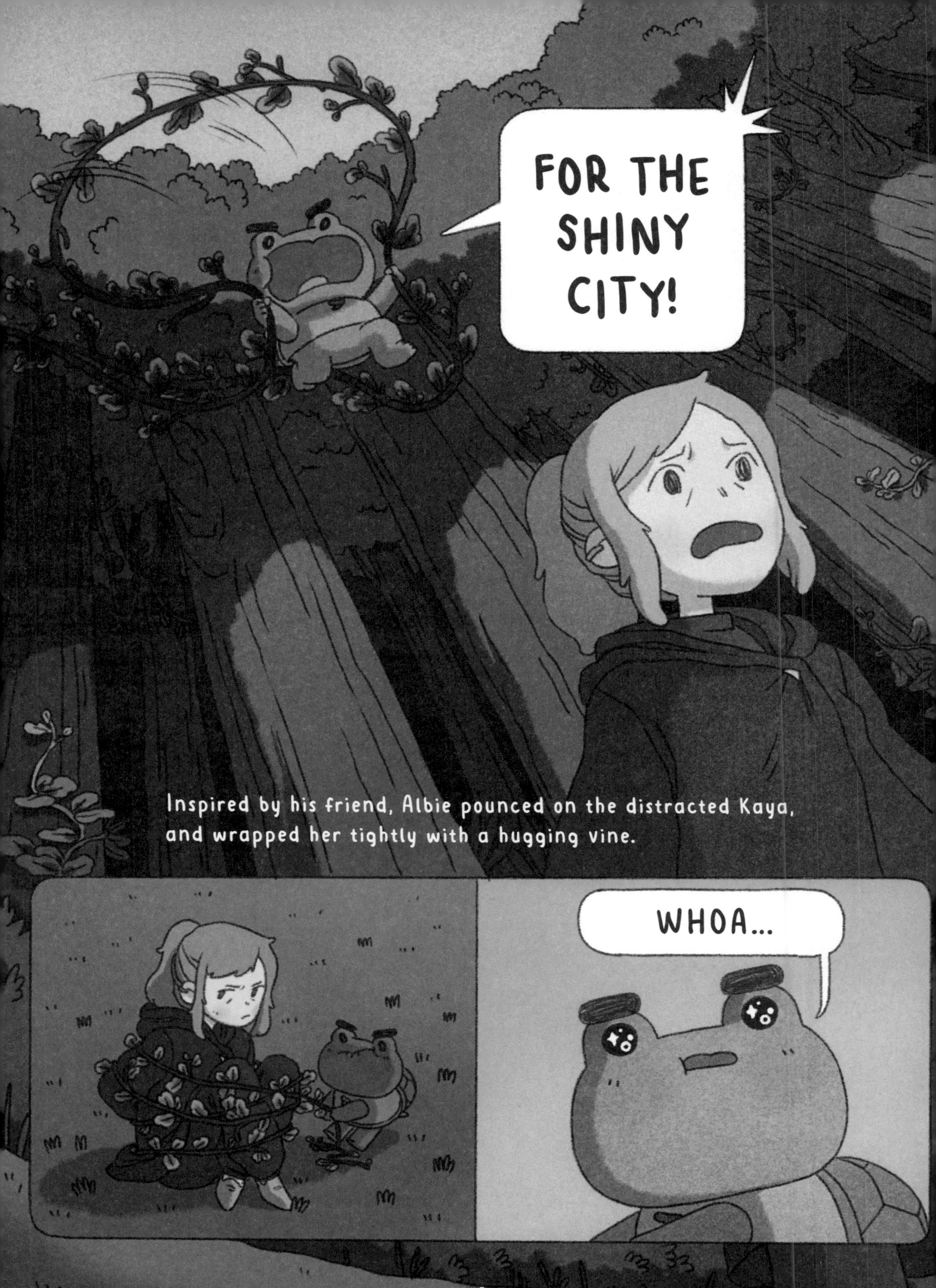
FOR THE SHINY CITY!
Inspired by his friend, Albie pounced on the distracted Kaya, and wrapped her tightly with a hugging vine.
WHOA...

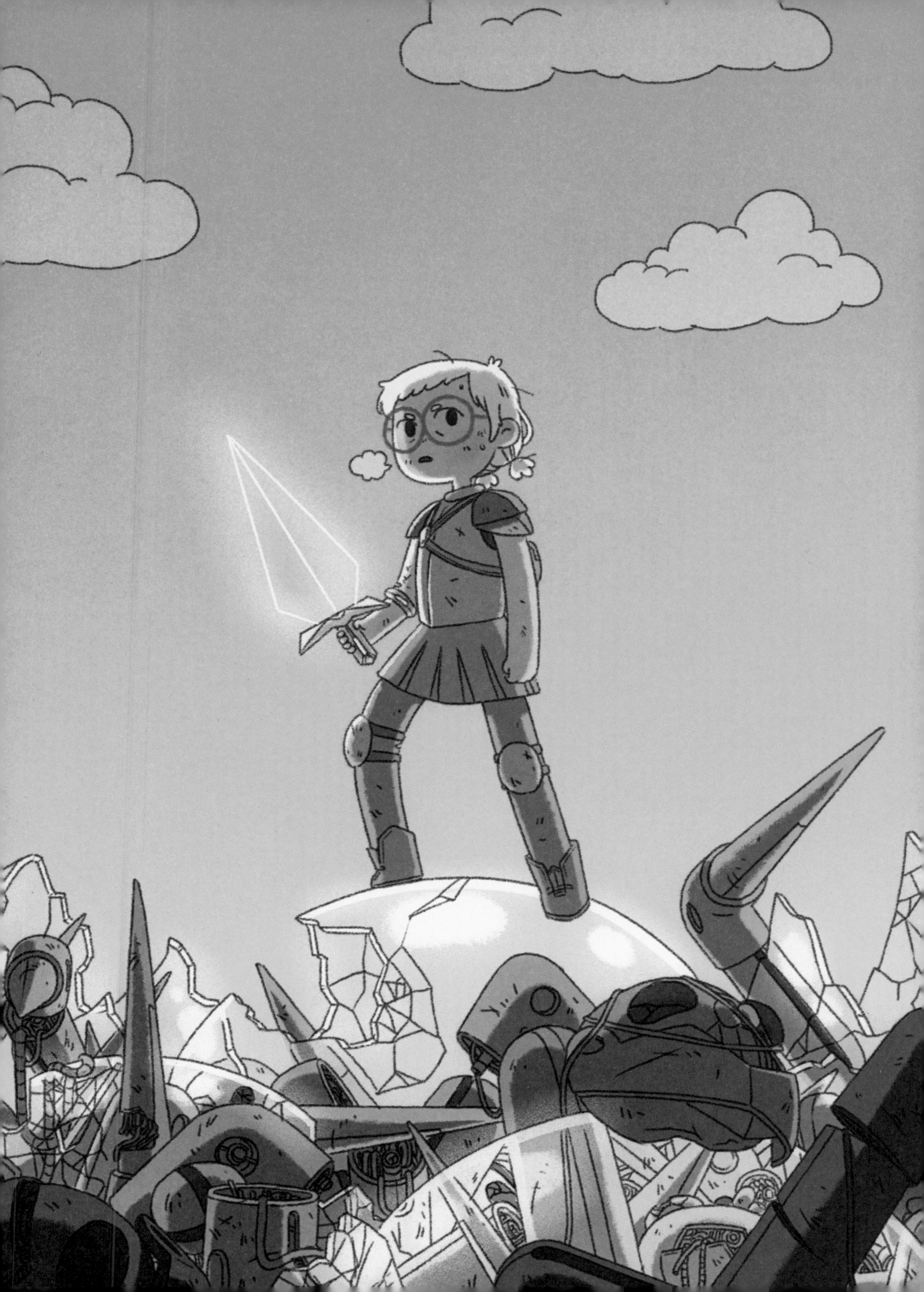

Juniper and Albie were very proud of each other.
They'd been just as bold and strong as Guardian Knights.

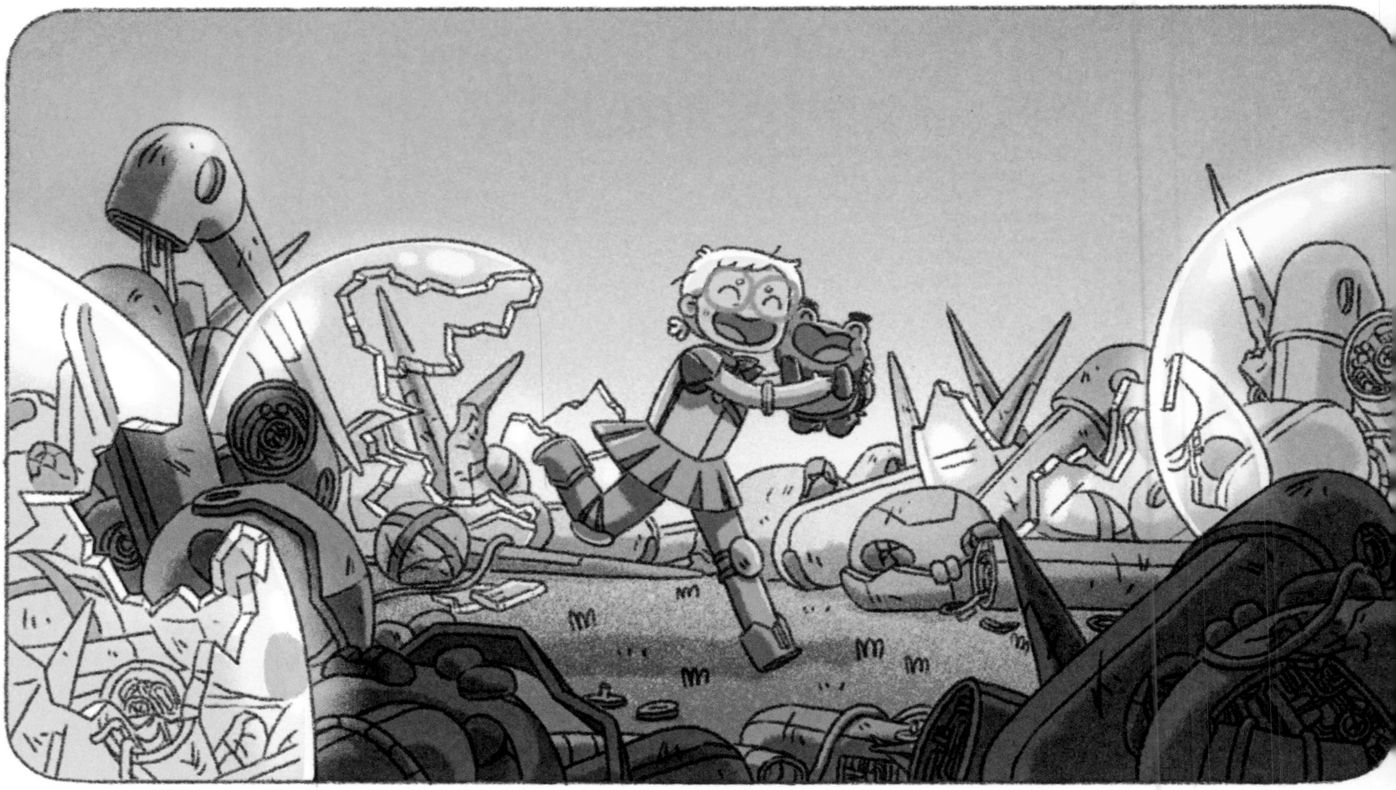

But there was still one problem: how were they going to get The Core's power back to the city?

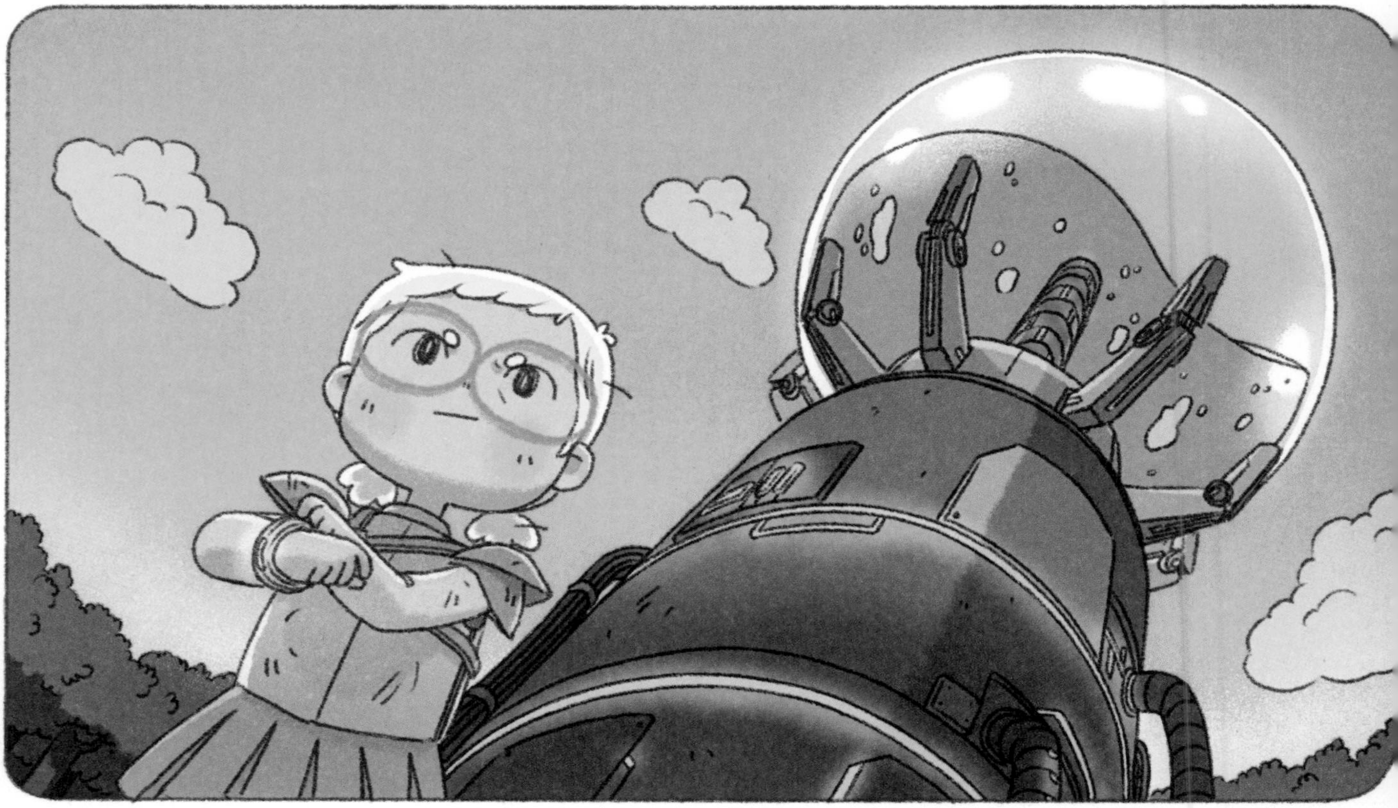

Then an idea struck Juniper.

Reusing Kaya's machinery, Juniper began to build. With Albie's help, she managed to assemble a device to store The Core's power: a containment orb for Kaya...

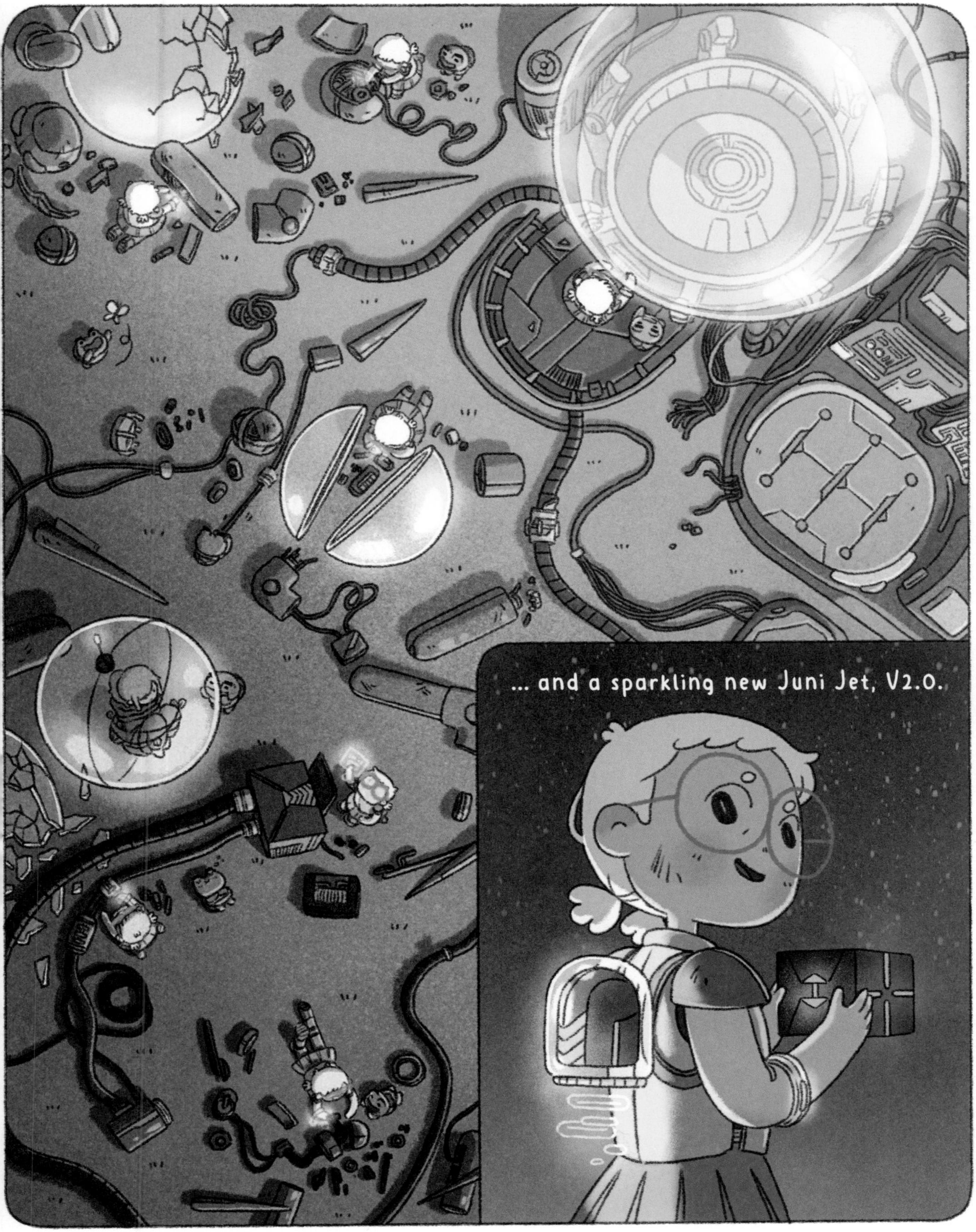
... and a sparkling new Juni Jet, V2.0.

As they jetted off, Albie shut his eyes and clung to Juniper at first, but soon realized he loved the feeling of the wind whizzing past him.

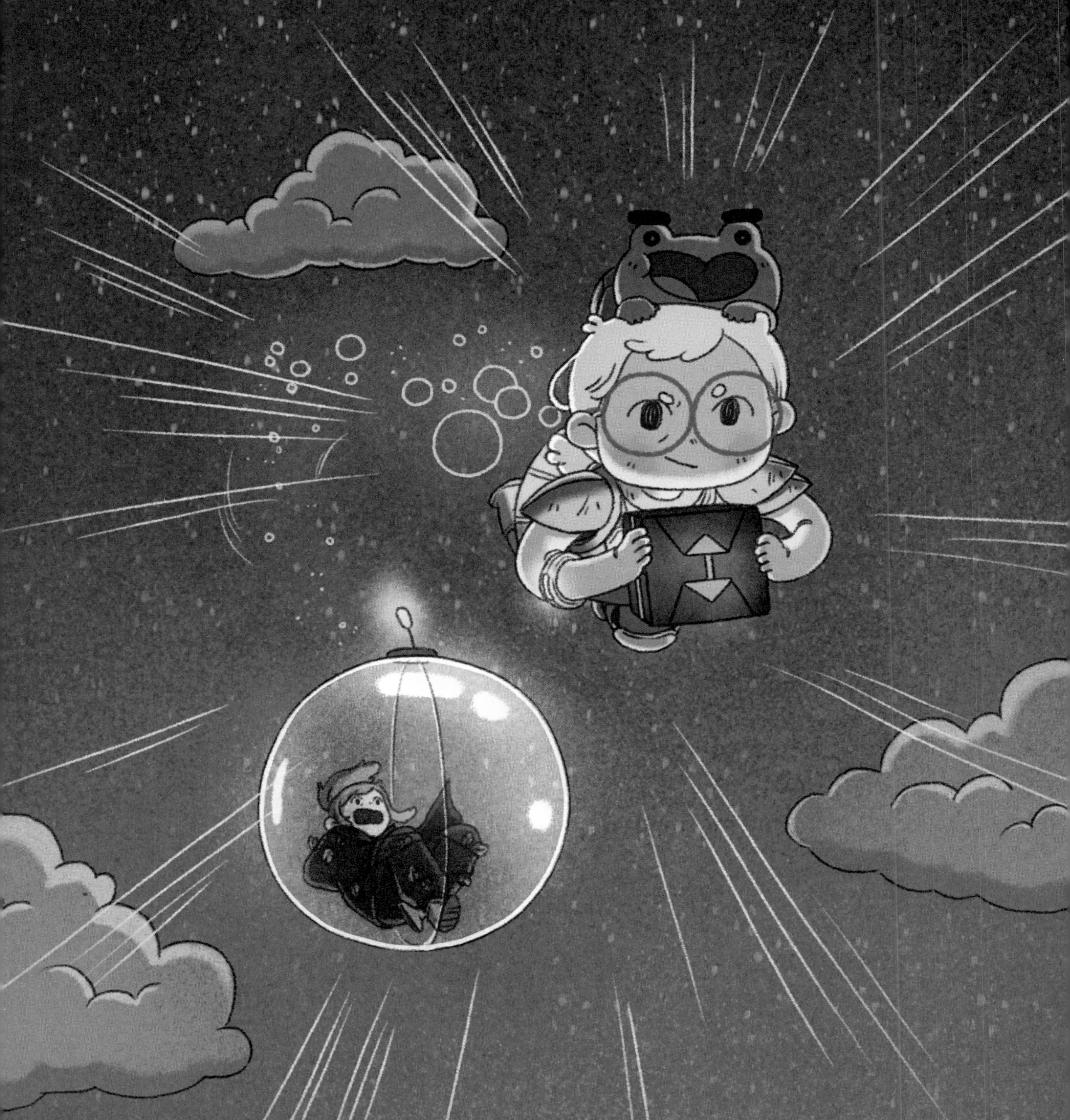

Juniper was in complete control this time, dipping and diving through the city with ease. But as they approached The Core, her face grew serious. They had a city to save.

The young inventor knew she only had one shot—she had to get this right. Her heart was beating so hard she could hear its pounding over the roar of the Juni Jet. She readied the built-in slingshot and aimed for the centre of The Core.

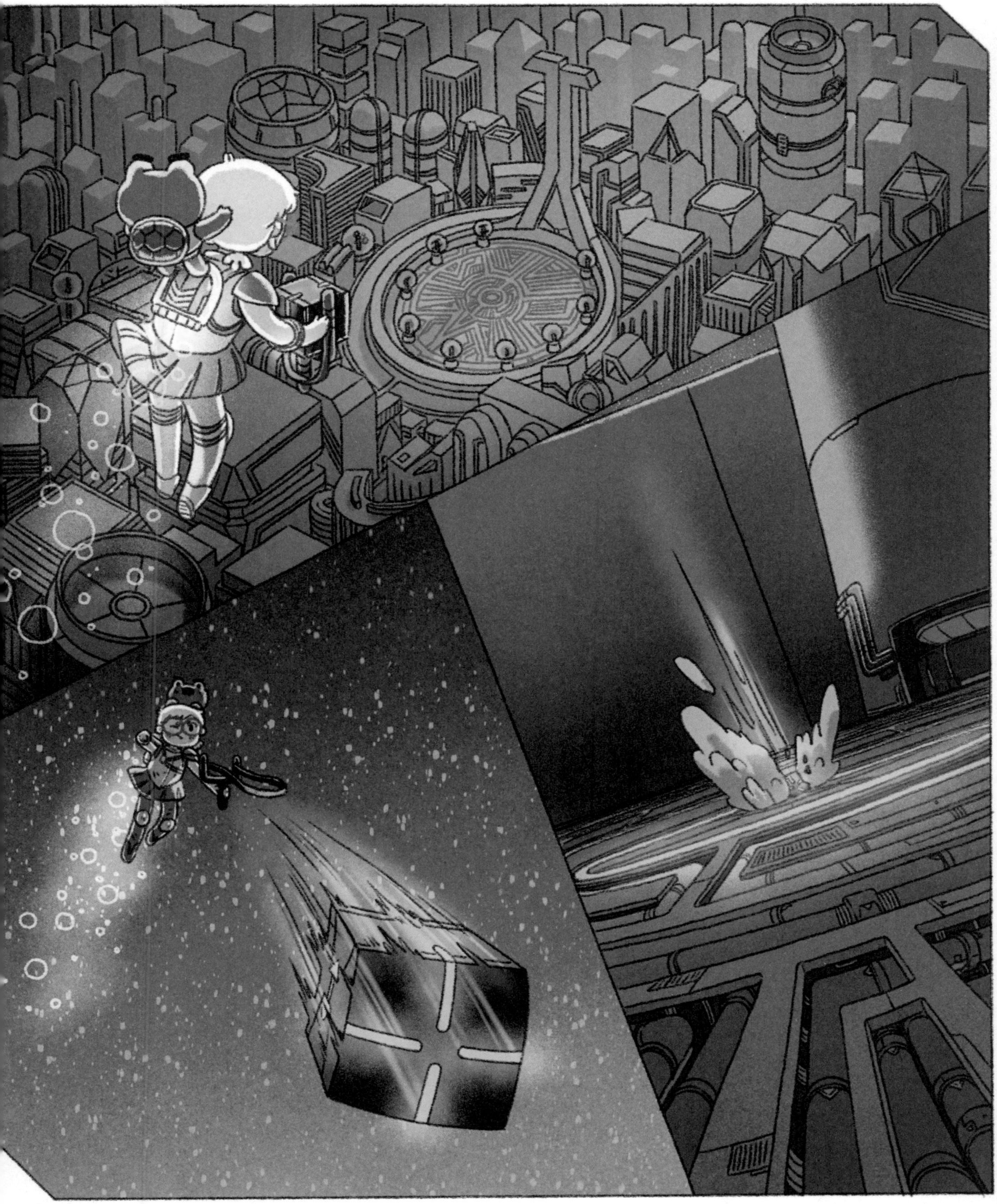

Tykotech City blossomed into light once more, and Juniper and Albie sighed with relief.

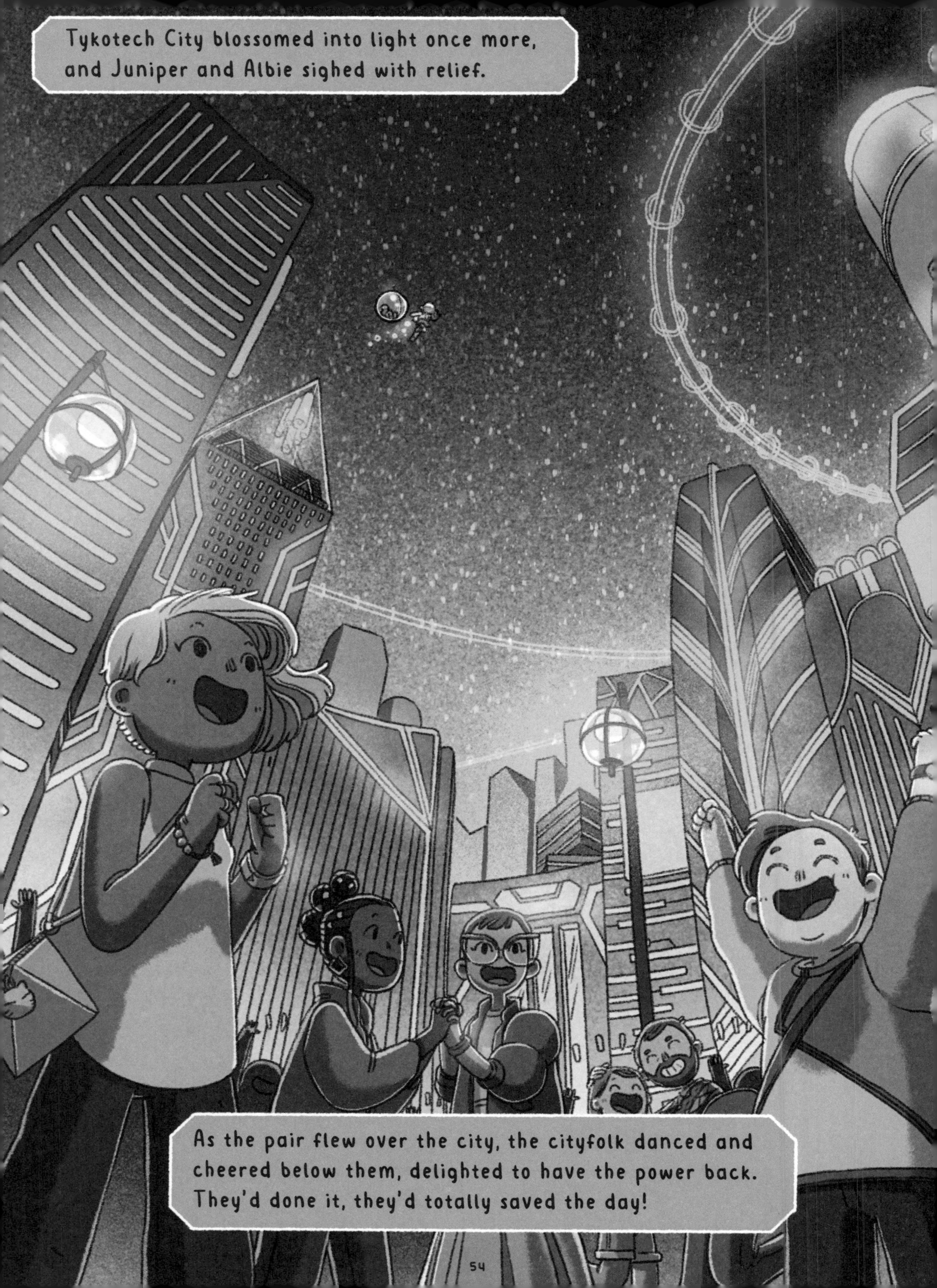

As the pair flew over the city, the cityfolk danced and cheered below them, delighted to have the power back. They'd done it, they'd totally saved the day!

etting the Kozen family mansion as its destination, Juniper turned on the utopilot on Kaya's containment orb. As it glided off, Juniper hoped there as still a chance Kaya and her mom could work things out.

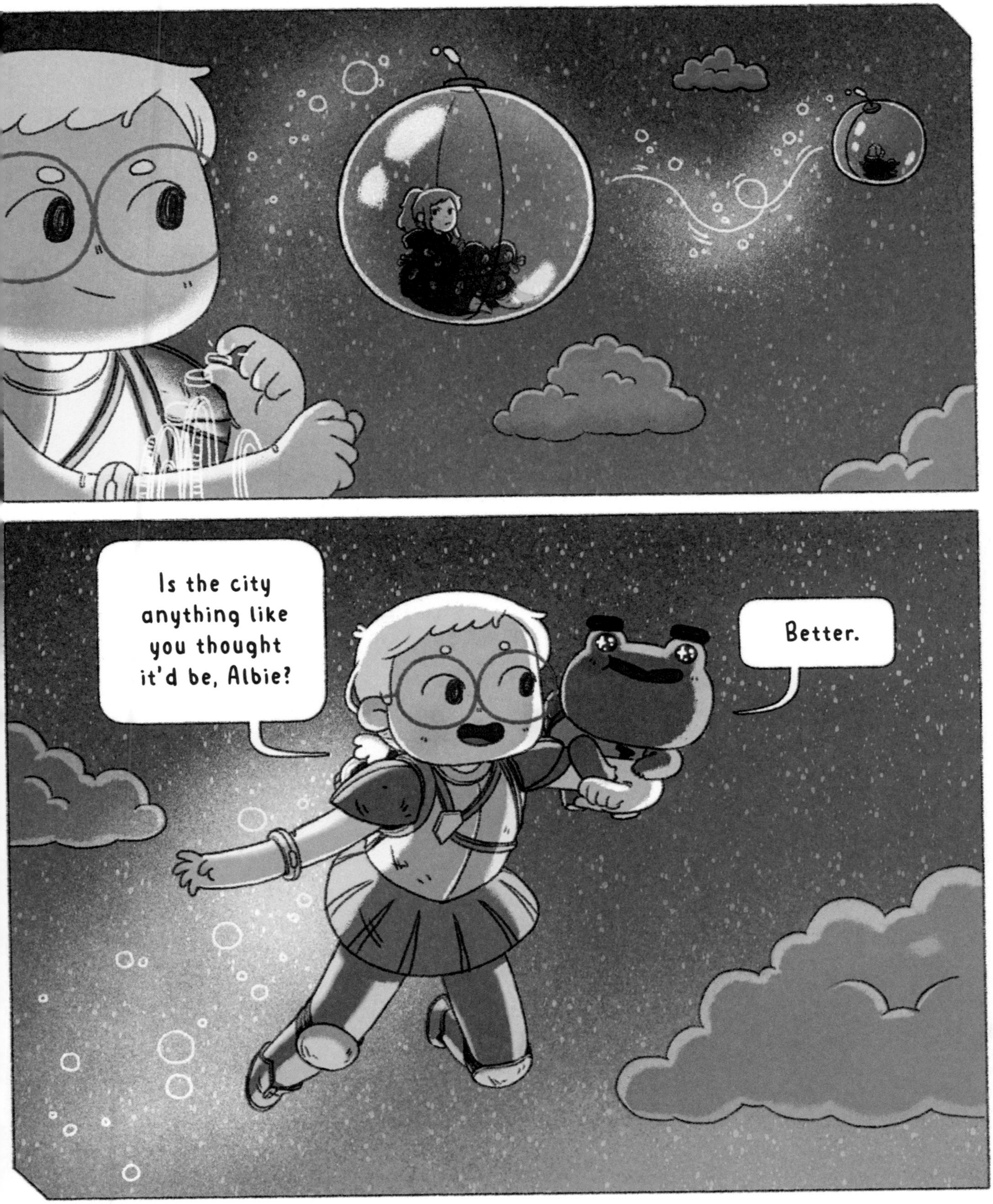
Is the city anything like you thought it'd be, Albie?
Better.

But then Juniper's heart sank as she thought of her dad and grandpa worrying about her at home—they hadn't seen her since before the bug-bot invasion.

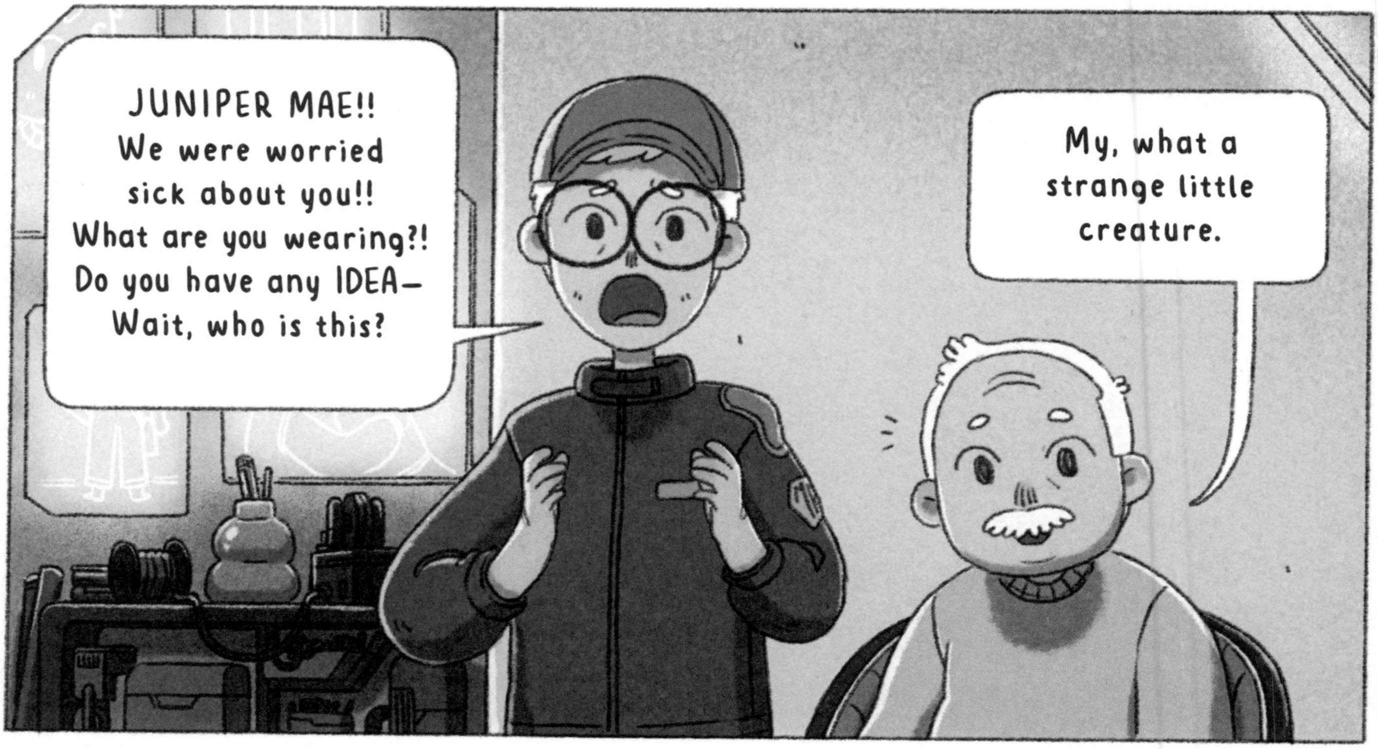
JUNIPER MAE!! We were worried sick about you!! What are you wearing?! Do you have any IDEA— Wait, who is this?
My, what a strange little creature.

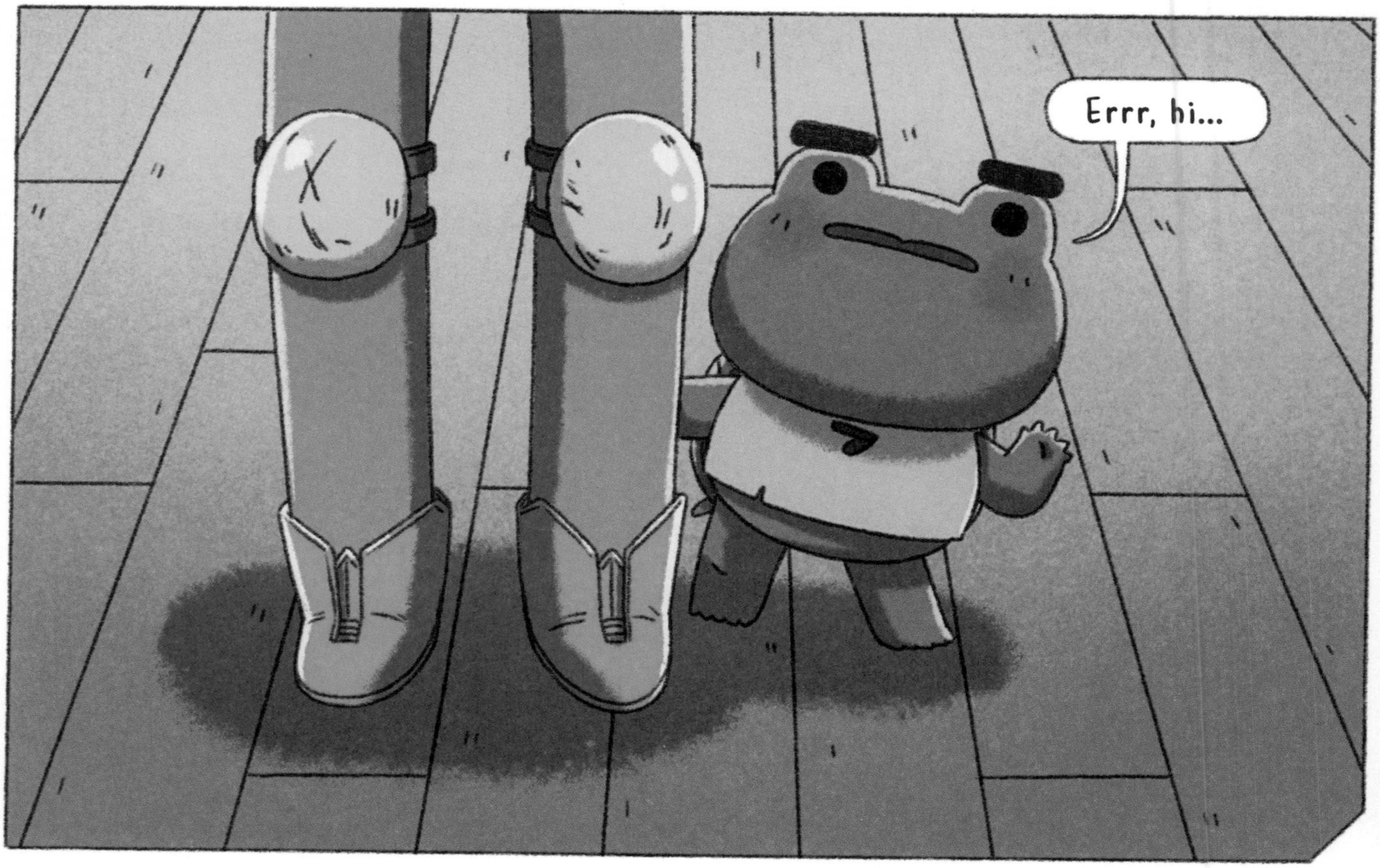
Errr, hi...

And so Juniper and Albie sat down with Mr Mae and Grandpa Mae and told them all about their adventures.

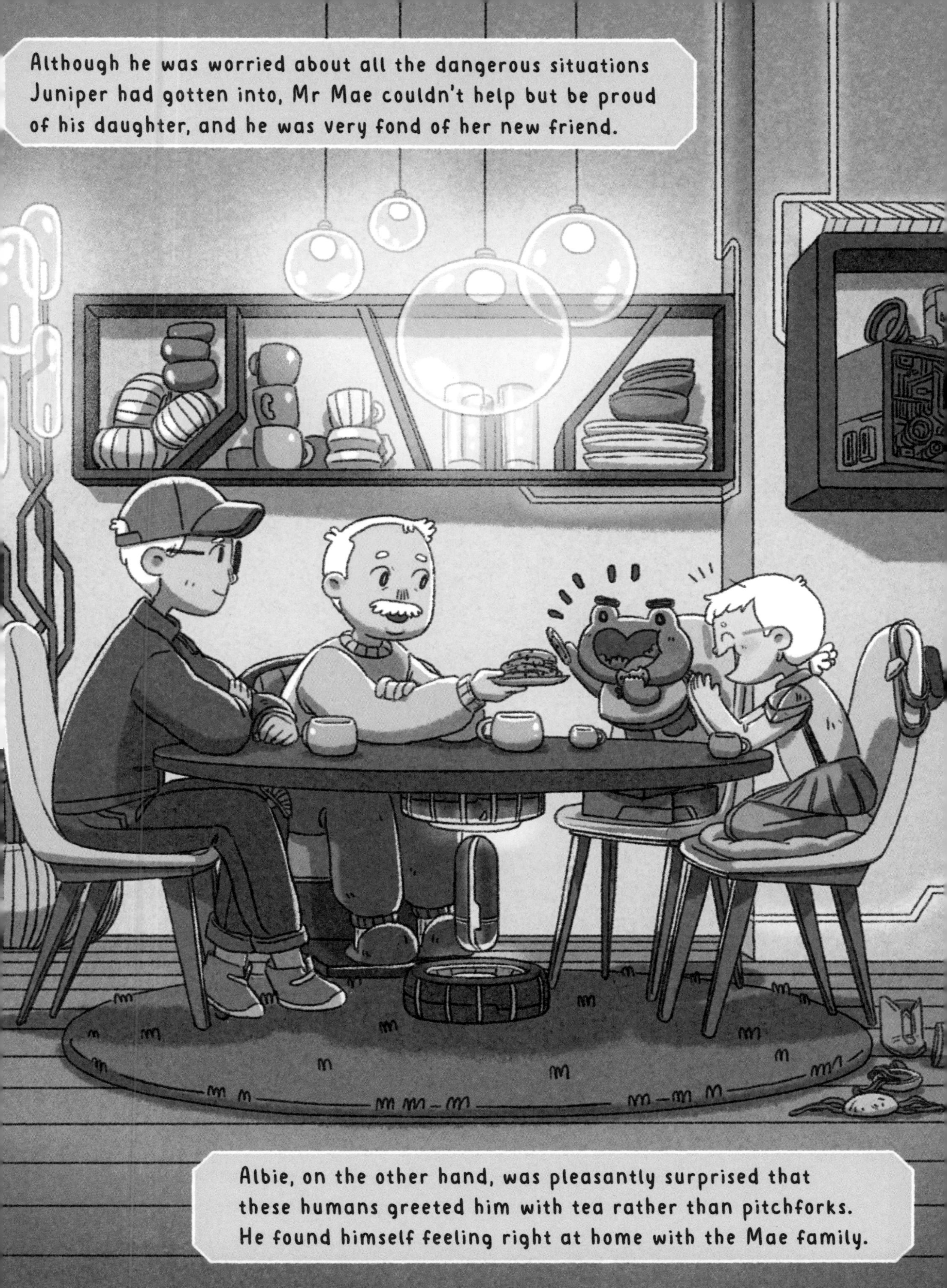
Although he was worried about all the dangerous situations Juniper had gotten into, Mr Mae couldn't help but be proud of his daughter, and he was very fond of her new friend.
Albie, on the other hand, was pleasantly surprised that these humans greeted him with tea rather than pitchforks. He found himself feeling right at home with the Mae family.

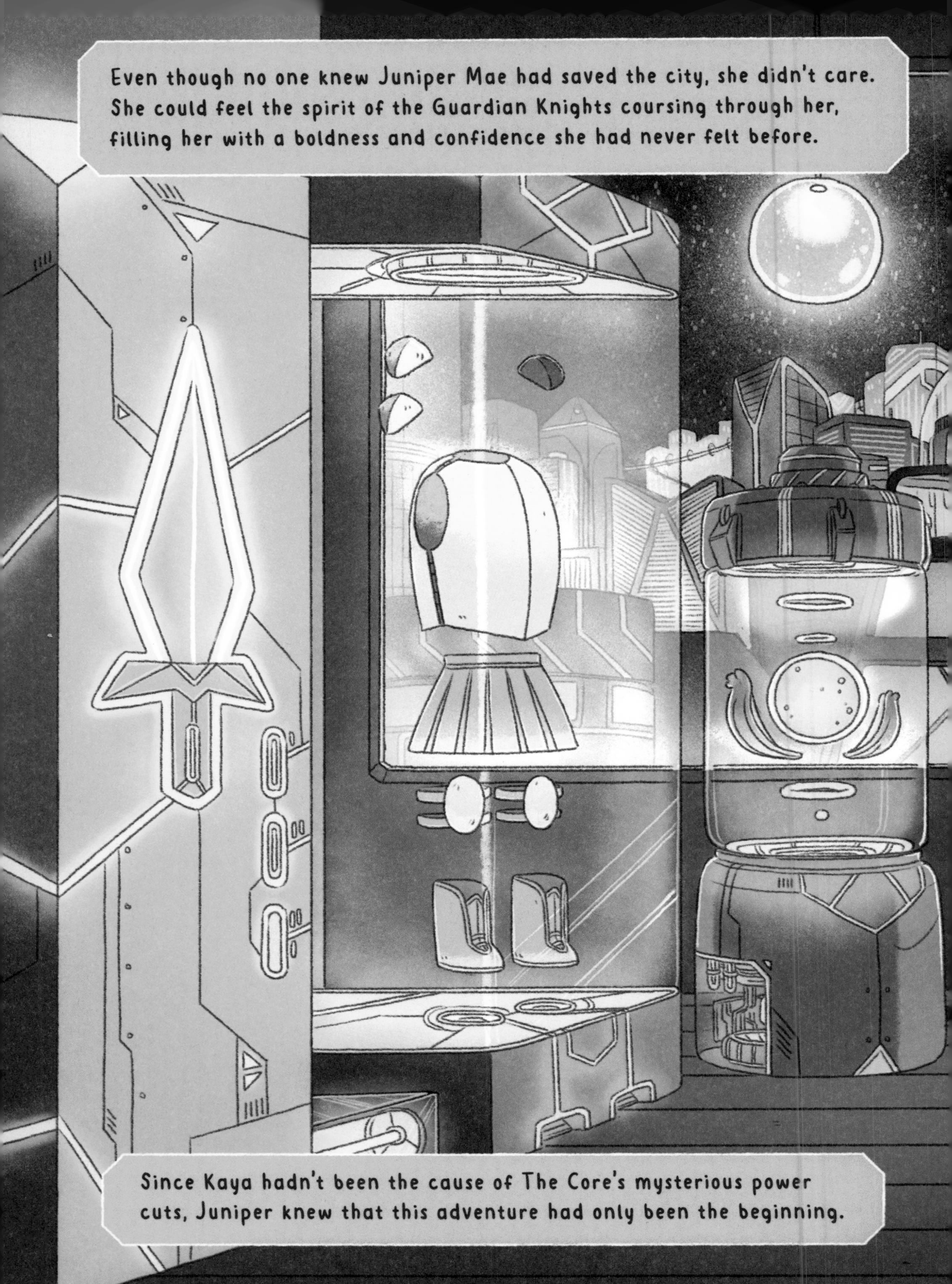
Even though no one knew Juniper Mae had saved the city, she didn't care. She could feel the spirit of the Guardian Knights coursing through her, filling her with a boldness and confidence she had never felt before.
Since Kaya hadn't been the cause of The Core's mysterious power cuts, Juniper knew that this adventure had only been the beginning.

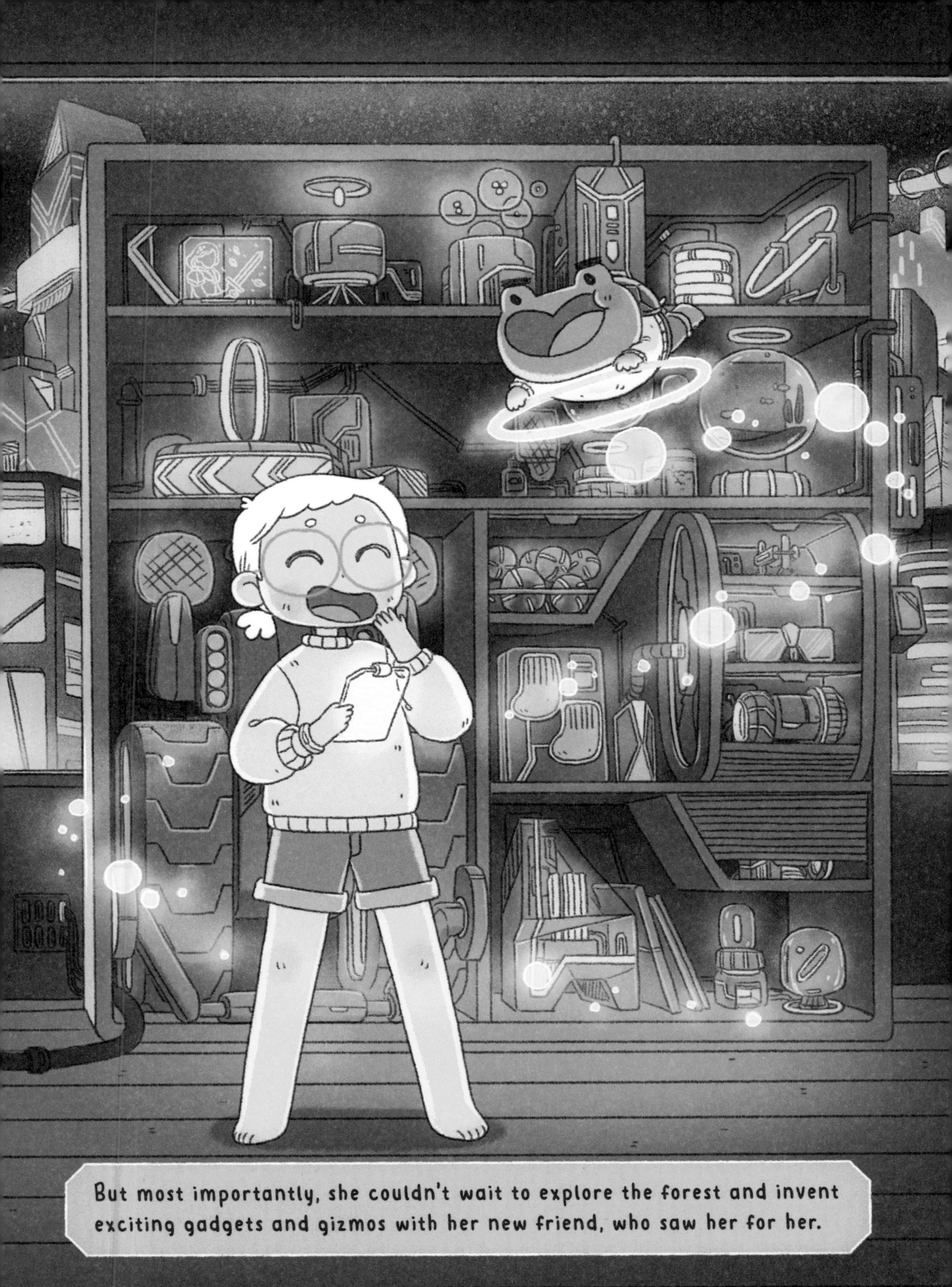

But most importantly, she couldn't wait to explore the forest and invent exciting gadgets and gizmos with her new friend, who saw her for her.

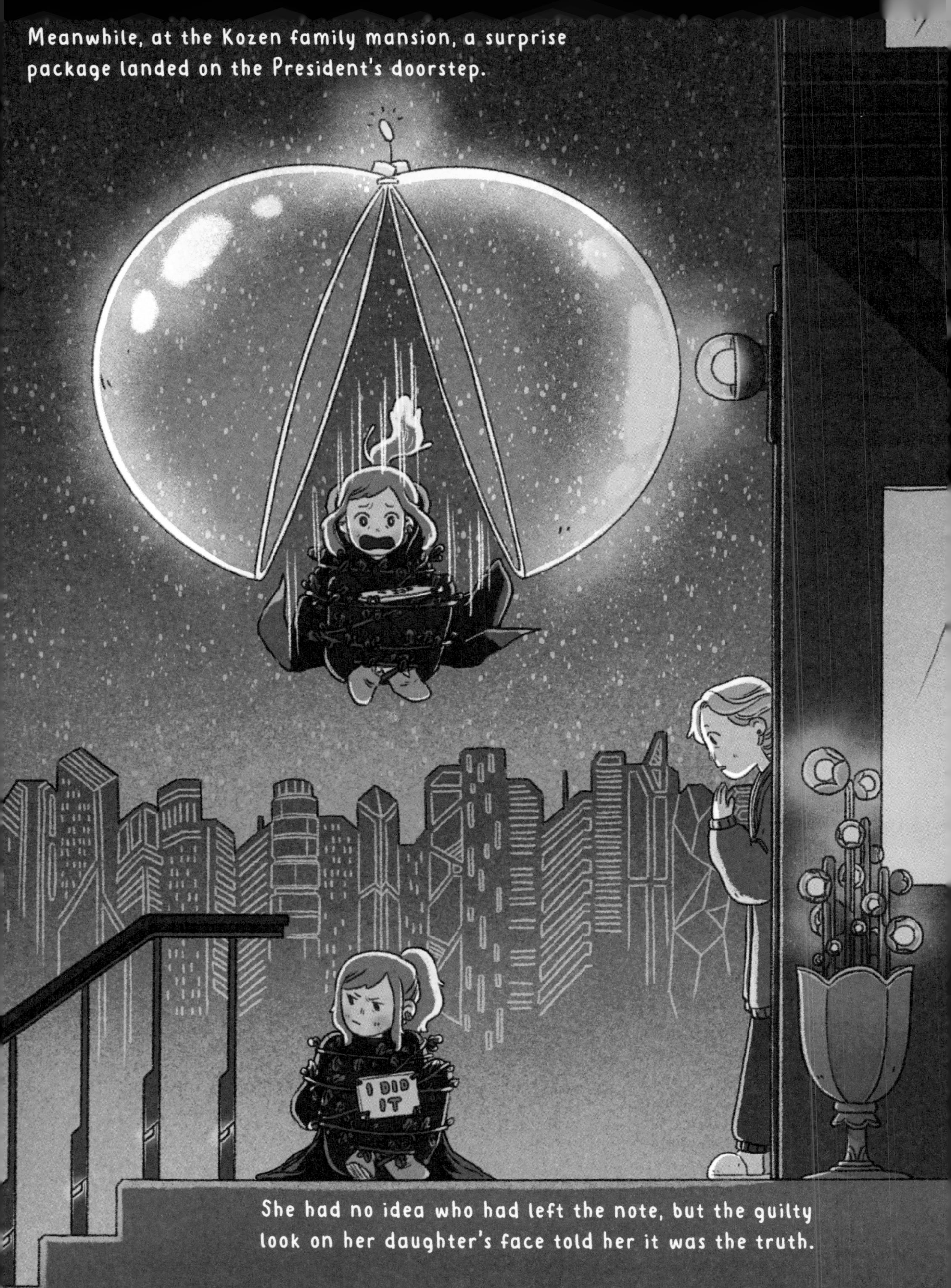
Meanwhile, at the Kozen family mansion, a surprise package landed on the President's doorstep.
I DID IT
She had no idea who had left the note, but the guilty look on her daughter's face told her it was the truth.

hat night, a grumpy, grounded Kaya had a visitor.

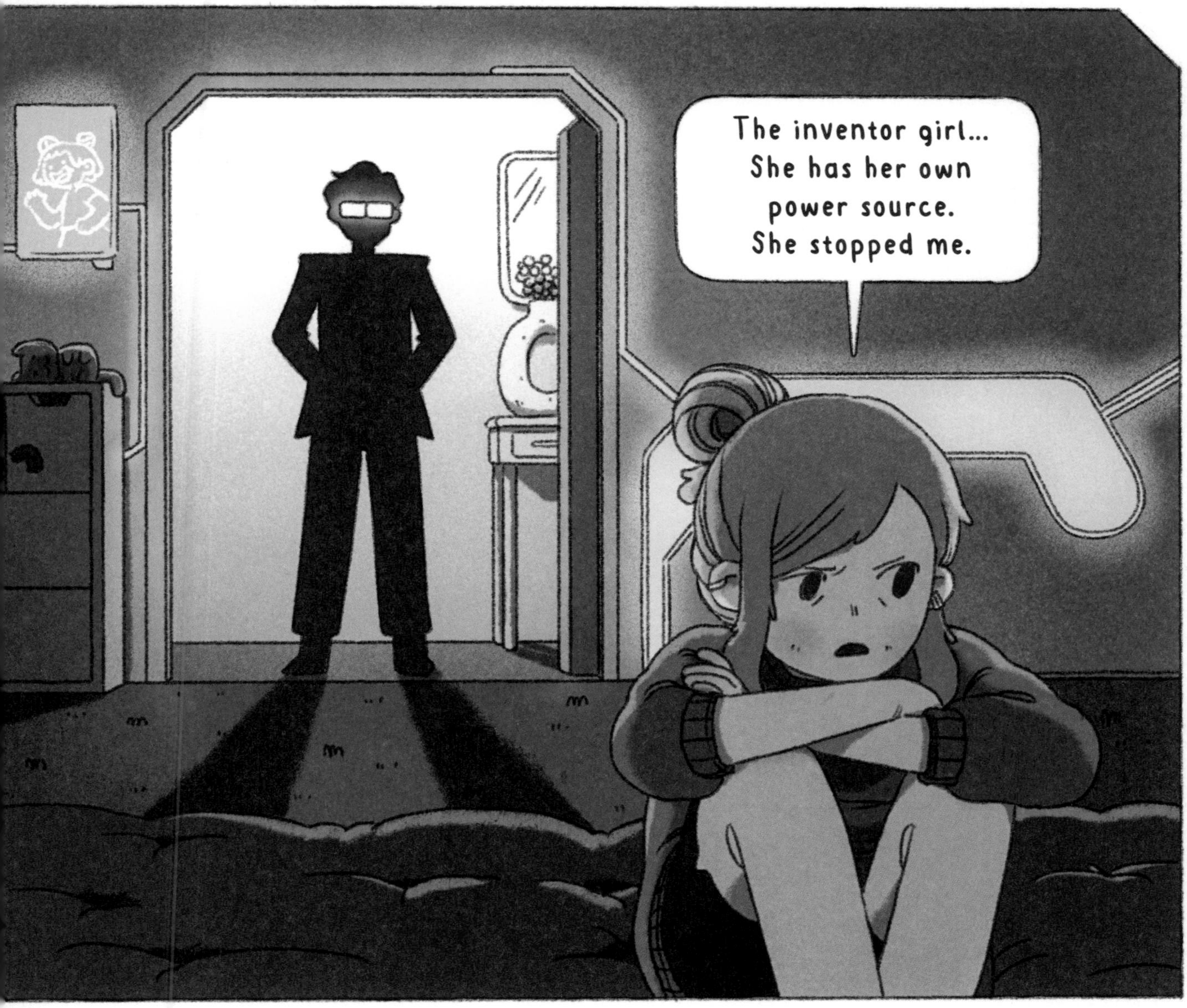
The inventor girl... She has her own power source. She stopped me.

For a moment, there was a long silence. Then, Kaya felt a cold shiver run down her spine as a deep, gravelly voice spoke up.

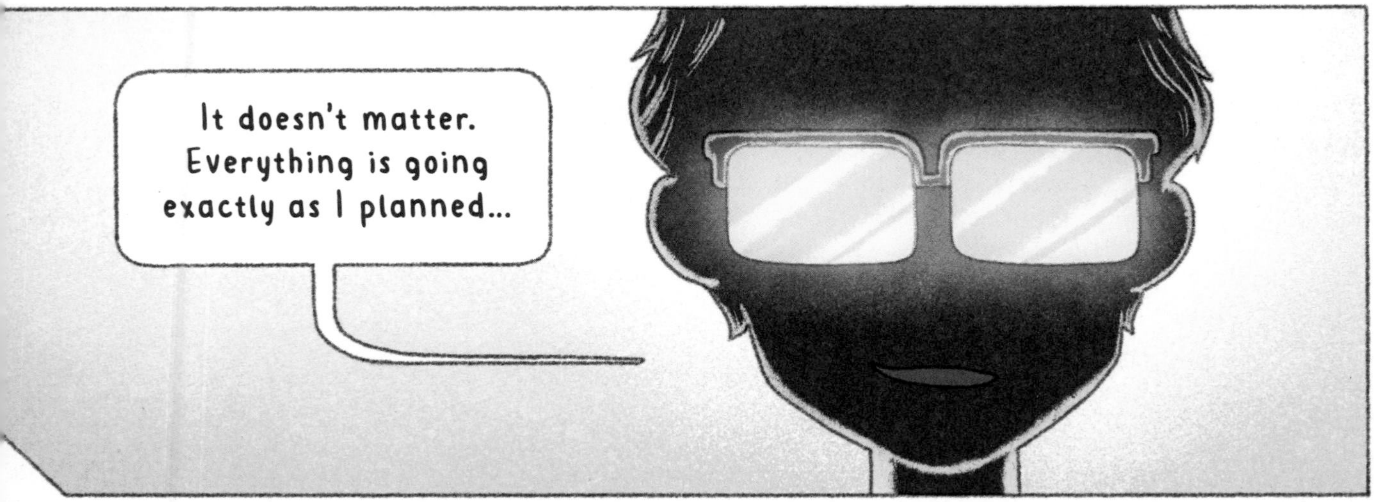
It doesn't matter. Everything is going exactly as I planned...

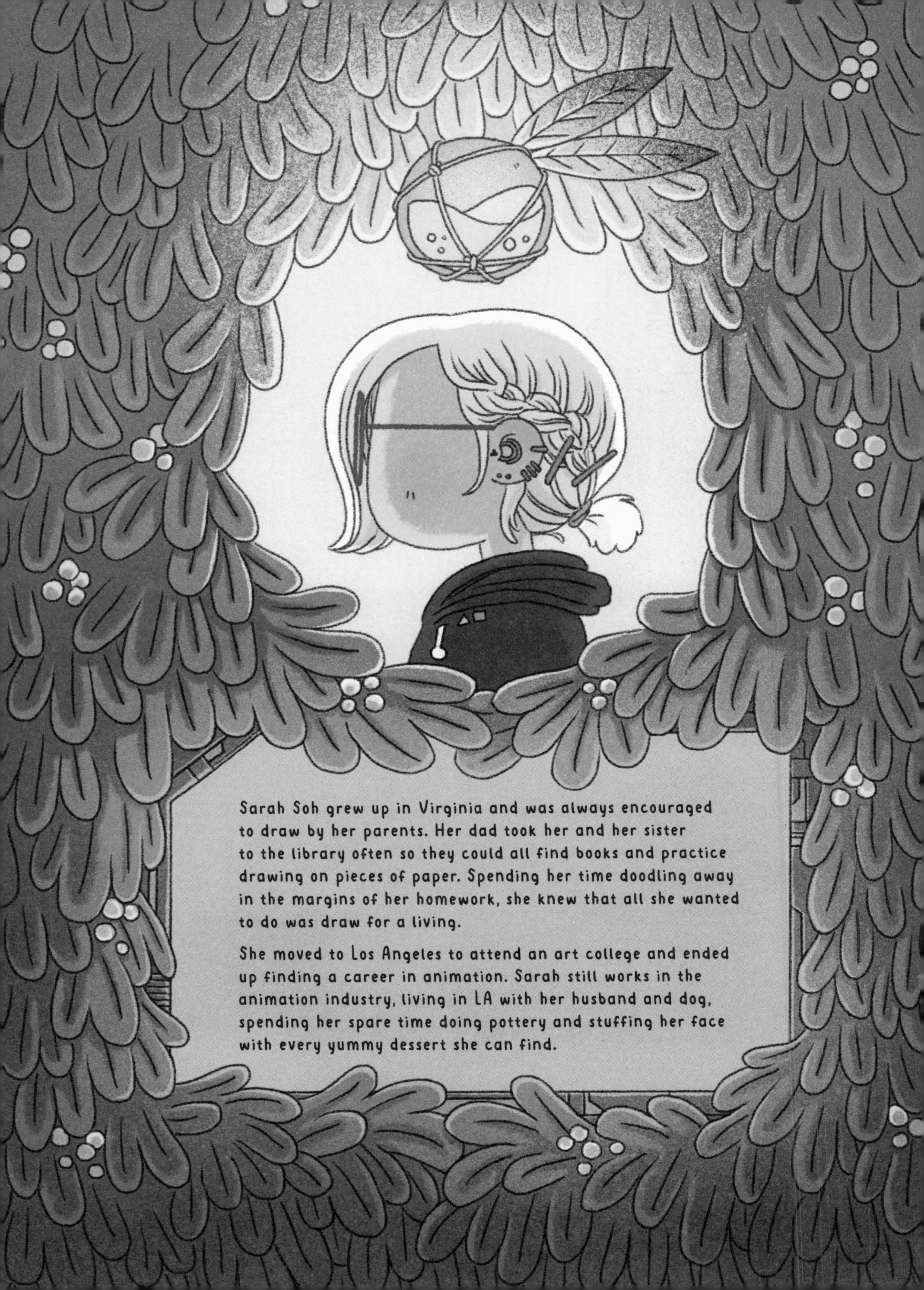

Sarah Soh grew up in Virginia and was always encouraged to draw by her parents. Her dad took her and her sister to the library often so they could all find books and practice drawing on pieces of paper. Spending her time doodling away in the margins of her homework, she knew that all she wanted to do was draw for a living.

She moved to Los Angeles to attend an art college and ended up finding a career in animation. Sarah still works in the animation industry, living in LA with her husband and dog, spending her spare time doing pottery and stuffing her face with every yummy dessert she can find.

JUNIPER MAE WILL RETURN...

Deep in the forest, Juniper Mae and Albie are working hard to become Guardian Knights. Training with greatswords, inventing dazzling new gadgets, befriending tama-tamas, and discovering ancient Guardian Knight artifacts is everything Juniper hoped it would be—but a great darkness is rising once again. Can the duo work to overcome some of their toughest opponents yet and protect their forest?

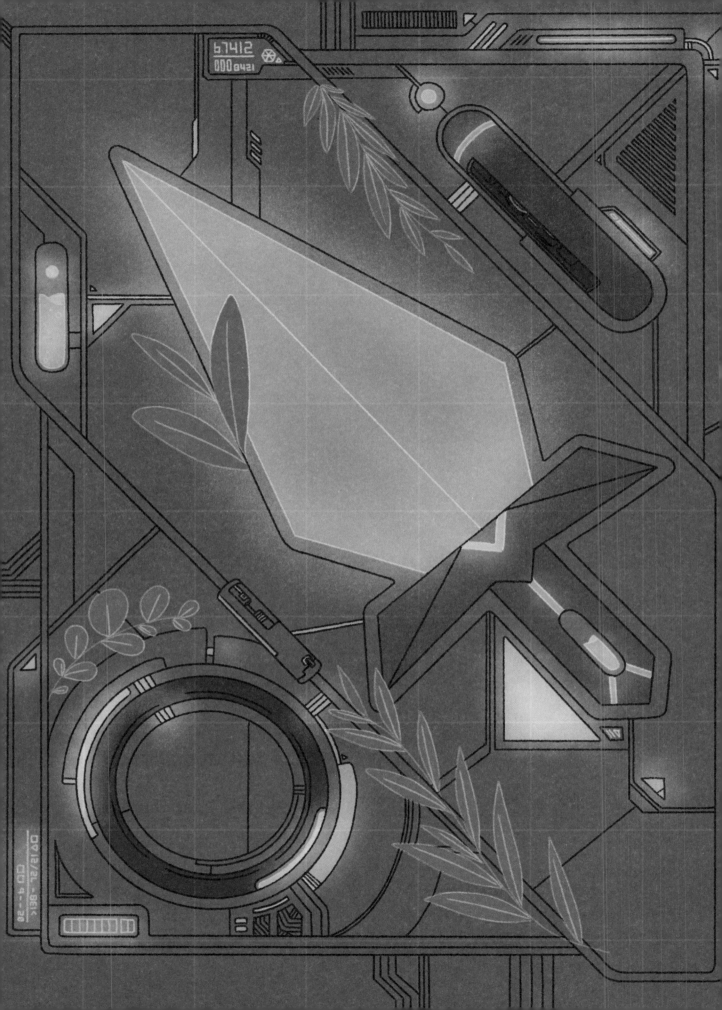